Came a Spider

Came a Spider

by Edward Levy

ARBOR HOUSE
New York

To my wife, Carole—
for believing in me at a time when I
needed her most.

Came a Spider

Chapter 1

SHE STOOD on a flat, sandy rock, sensing the area around her. Nothing moved in the bright moonlight except a tiny caravan of insects rooting in the sand. The soft breeze moving across the desert floor ruffled the thick brown hair on her body but brought her sensing organs —nothing.

She moved backward into the shadow from an overhang in the rocks, and continued to digest her meal. The shriveled remains of the kangaroo rat she had just devoured lay in the sand, the ants curiously inspecting what was left of it.

1

She was extremely large for a spider. Her fat, hairy body being almost three inches in length, her legs extending another four. Her large head moved slightly as she rotated her mouth parts, getting the last traces of food from the tufts of hair around her fangs. She could not be seen in the shadow as she stood motionless; only her eyes, glowing like little coals from the bright moonlight, could be seen.

She was unique for a spider. Her ancestors had been common tarantulas—she was much larger than they had been, more vicious; her instincts were different. No spider who ever walked the earth was quite like her.

A RIFLE shot broke the stillness, the jackrabbit fell over in its tracks with a bullet through its brain. Lee Miller lowered the rifle and walked silently through the sand and over the rocks to where the rabbit had fallen, his eyes alert and watching for any movement.

It was great fun to be fifteen years old and go out hunting. Dad had bought him the .22 for his birthday, along with new hiking boots and camping gear. Dad and his brother Steve had spent most of today showing him how to properly aim and fire the rifle; now he had gotten his first rabbit with it. Dad had wanted them all to hunt together, but he had insisted on going out on his own. Now he was glad that he did. Dad would be proud of him.

As he crossed the desert sand, heading toward the rabbit he had gotten, he still found himself wondering about the chain-link fence he had seen before. Imagine, a high chain-link fence, stretching as far as he could see in both directions, right out here in the middle of nowhere. He had been greatly tempted to climb the fence and see what there was over the small rise inside, but the RESTRICTED GOVERNMENT PROPERTY—NO TRESPASSING signs that hung from the fence about every hundred

2

yards quickly changed his mind. Dad had always taught him never to trespass on someone else's land, that he could get into a lot of trouble. He had detoured in another direction, away from the fence. Then he had spotted his rabbit. But he still couldn't help wondering what the government would need with barren, deserted land like this, out here in the middle of nowhere.

His dog, who had been sniffing around up ahead, began barking crazily. "Joker!" he shouted. "Stop that barking and come here!" He stooped to pick up the rabbit, then put it in his game bag. "Joker! Come on, you stupid dog!" he called again, but the shepherd kept running around and barking excitedly at something hiding between the rocks of a small hill. "Whatcha got, boy?" he asked as he reached the dog. "Another rabbit?"

He knelt down to have a look, but all he could see was a dark shape crouching in the space between the rocks. Then it came out, its fangs spread and ready, its front legs raised high in a fighting position. It moved forward slightly, its fat, hairy body held tensely, quickly changing its position with every move the boy made, meeting him squarely.

"*Damn,*" Lee said, amazed. "Look at the size of that thing." He grabbed the dog by the collar. "Get back, boy."

The dog tore himself from the boy's grip, and with the hair on the back of his neck standing high, and barking excitedly, he circled the . . . spider, darting forward with a growl, then jumping back to circle again.

The boy was fascinated by the size of the spider. What he had thought was just a curious marking he could now see was the small numerals 86, painted in white across the spider's back. Damn, he thought. He just had to show this one to dad.

He pulled his hunting knife from the leather scabbard

he wore on his belt and poked gingerly at it, trying to force it back against the rock, where he could succeed in getting it trapped and imprisoned in his game bag. He leaned forward slightly, resting his left hand on the rock to support his weight, and tried slipping the knife blade under the spider to lift it.

There was a blur of movement as the spider shot forward, digging the sharp claws on each of its legs deep into the boy's forearm. With a cry, the boy straightened up and shook his arm violently, trying to dislodge the spider. It held fast, again and again sinking its fangs into the boy's soft flesh, injecting more venom each time.

With his free hand Lee grabbed the spider and pulled hard, but the spider held on. From the underside of its abdomen the spider produced a short, stingerlike protrusion and jabbed it deep into the boy's arm; its entire body seemed to shudder.

Lee screamed as a white-hot pain ran up his arm, numbing it. He pulled again on the spider, using all the strength he could muster. This time it came loose, leaving behind deep gouges where its claws had been ripped from the flesh. Lee threw the spider down hard against the side of the rock. Immediately it righted itself and charged forward again, trying to attack the boy's leg. He stomped quickly with his boot and caught the spider squarely, crushing it into the hard-packed sand by the rock, leaving a large smear of cream-colored goo where its body had been. The legs jerked and twitched spasmodically. Lee stomped the spider again to make sure it was dead.

His arm throbbed painfully and was bleeding. In the center of the gouges made by the spider's claws rose a large purple blister the size of a half dollar. His shirt was soaked with perspiration and his head spun dizzily. He shook it to try to clear it, and his vision cleared somewhat, but he was still dizzy and was beginning to feel nauseated. He tried taking a few steps but the nausea was getting worse. Finally, when he could control it no longer, he bent forward and, dropping to his knees, vomited. After what seemed an eternity of stomach-wrenching contractions, they subsided and he began to feel better.

He picked up his rifle where he had dropped it, gathered up his knife and game bag, and started walking slowly. His legs felt so heavy he could hardly lift them; it took all of his willpower to keep from stumbling in the soft sand.

"Come on, Joker," he called weakly. "Let's—let's go find dad. I—I don't feel so good."

He started back the way they had come, the dog scampering ahead, sniffing everything in sight, occasionally peeing on a likely looking cactus or the side of a rock.

Lee looked at his painfully throbbing arm. It was bleeding steadily from the deep wounds, the blood leaving a little trail in the sand behind him as he walked. He stopped and, reaching down with shaking fingers, unlaced the leather bootlace from his right boot. Tying the leather thong tightly around his injured left arm just above his elbow, then breaking off a small twig from a bush, he inserted it under the thong and gave it a half twist. The bleeding stopped. He began walking again, holding the makeshift tourniquet in place with his good hand.

He got as far as the second rise before a rush of dizziness caught up with him. His knees turned to rubber. He fell forward, sprawling, face in the sand. He tried to pick himself up again and managed to make it to his hands and knees before his strength gave out completely. He fell back again, the sand gritting between his teeth. He vaguely felt movement near him as the dog came back to

5

investigate, lay down beside him and, whining softly, licked the sand from his face.

HARRY MILLER huddled closer to the open fire in an effort to warm himself against the chill of the night desert air. He looked at his watch for the third time in the last ten minutes. "I'm getting worried, Steve," he said to his older son. "That kid should have been back three hours ago."

"Take it easy, dad," Steve said. "Lee's a big boy now and he knows how to take care of himself." He moved closer to the fire to warm his hands.

Harry got up from his squatting position by the fire, stretching the cramps out of his legs. He walked over to the front of the camper and squinted, trying to see out into the dark desert landscape. No signs of movement; he could hear nothing. He stretched again and rubbed his eyes. It had been a long day. "Get the flashlights, Steve, and grab a rifle. We can't just sit around and do nothing. The kid might be hurt—"

"Dad, you don't have to—"

"Do what I tell you. I know the desert; things can happen out there."

Harry started out across the desert in the direction he knew his son had gone. Reluctantly, Steve got the flashlights and a rifle from the rear of the camper, hurried after him.

Harry had no trouble following the trail of his son and the dog, and he had a moment of panic as he saw that his son's trail was leading directly toward the fenced area. He wouldn't! he thought to himself as he read the warning sign. He'd know better than to go in there. He felt relief as the trail veered sharply to the right across the open desert again.

Within another twenty minutes he could see the dog

6

running in circles and barking excitedly. And then he saw Lee, curled up in a ball in the sand. He broke into a run, stumbling and tripping over the rocks and brush.

He reached his son and dropped to his knees. Lee was breathing heavily, but nothing seemed broken. Harry cradled his son's head in his lap and thanked God the boy was alive.

Steve came running up. "What happened to him, is he dead—?"

"What the hell kind of talk is that? No, he's not dead. He just got hurt somehow—and I think he's in shock."

Lee's eyelids fluttered, opened. "Dad, I didn't—you find—bit by spider . . ."

"Don't try to talk, we'll get you home, then you can tell me all about it."

"God, look at his *arm*," Steve said, turning one of the flashlights on it. "Looks like he got bitten by something . . ."

For the first time Harry noticed his son's wounded arm. It was swollen and bruised and slightly discolored. The blood had congealed around the deep gashes and it was caked with sand. Some small ants were crawling on it. He carefully brushed them off, then released the tourniquet; blood immediately began flowing from the wounds again. He waited a few seconds, then reapplied the tourniquet.

Harry got to his feet, looked around and saw the rifle lying in the sand. "That damned rifle. I never should have let the kid go out by himself with it . . ." He saw traces in the sand where his son had either crawled or rolled the last fifty yards. "That damned rifle . . ."

He carefully wrapped his coat around his son, then picked him up in his arms. "Come on, fella, let's get on home."

7

Chapter 2

JEAN MILLER stood by the side of the bed looking down at her son. A nervous, high-strung woman, she had nearly suffered an emotional collapse when Harry had carried her son, bleeding and incoherent, into the house. When Dr. Franklin arrived, he had to give her a shot to calm her even before he had a chance to examine her son.

Dr. Franklin jabbed a hypodermic needle into Lee's arm, and pressed the plunger slowly. He withdrew the needle, then returned it to his medical bag. "I've given him a mild tranquilizer," he said. "What he needs most right now is some sleep, but"—looking at Jean—"he'll be just fine, no need to worry. You've got a strong young man here. He's in a mild state of shock and is suffering some side effects from those nasty bites on his arm. I've taken a sample of blood from him and will have it analyzed. That should tell us if there are any traces of poison or venom in his system. It was quite a traumatic experience for him. Whatever it was he ran into out there on the desert scared him pretty badly."

Jean Miller looked down at her son again, sleeping now, his face pale and drawn, still mumbling under his breath about a spider. She saw the clean, white bandage covering the wounds on his left arm, and her hands began to shake again.

Dr. Franklin touched her elbow. "Let's leave him to rest now," he suggested. "I'll come back tomorrow morning to begin the treatments . . ."

They left Lee's bedroom and went down the hall to the living room, where Harry Miller was sitting on the couch, working on his third Scotch. "Well, how is he, doc?"

"Oh, he should be just fine—with rest, and the proper medication. I'll be back tomorrow morning to give him the first injection of the Pasteur treatment."

"Pasteur treatment? I thought that was for rabies. You don't get rabies from a spider."

"Harry," Dr. Franklin said, "the claw marks on Lee's arm measured eight inches in circumference. They stretch from his wrist to his elbow. Now tell me the truth —have you ever seen a spider that large?"

"Well, no, but I told you what Lee was mumbling out on the desert. All the way home in the camper I could hear him carrying on about a giant spider trying to eat him. He's in his room right now, still saying it was a spider—and I believe him."

"Well, in my opinion, your son was attacked by a large

rodent of some type. Probably a rat."

"A rat! Come on, doc! You counted the claw marks. Whoever heard of a goddamn rat with eight legs? And, anyhow, that's definitely a sting mark on his arm. Are you telling me rats have stingers on the end of their tails?"

"But, Harry," Jean put in, "neither do spiders."

Dr. Franklin took a deep breath. "Harry," he said calmly, "let's agree we aren't certain exactly what injured your son, but we must take every precaution. He's got to have those treatments. In the morning, after I get back the results of the blood test, I'll—"

"No!" Harry said emphatically. "I won't allow it. We can't put him through those terrible injections on pure speculation. He's been through *enough*."

Dr. Franklin picked up his medical bag again, preparing to leave. "Mr. Miller," he said formally, "I will not endanger the life of one of my patients because of ignorance—"

"Ignorance!"

"Yes, ignorance. If the blood test comes back showing what I suspect it will show—I'm prepared to get a court order if necessary. Your son will receive the treatment he needs."

"Harry, listen to me," Jean said, with a calmness she didn't feel. "You've been through a lot, you're upset, and you're not thinking clearly." She took his hand. "If the tests do show rabies, would you really deny Lee the treatment?"

"No, of course not."

She turned to the doctor. "And if the test is negative, we have nothing to worry about." She smiled at both of them. "Then, what the hell are you two arguing about?"

"I'll call you as soon as I get the results from the blood test," Dr. Franklin said simply. "Good night." He closed the door behind him.

"Harry, what do you think?" Jean asked, her fear returning.

He went to the bar and fixed himself another Scotch. "I think the kid'll be okay. I'm sure of it. He just had a bad time, but it won't be anything serious."

"Harry, are you sure?"

"I'm *sure,*" he said, hoping to god he was right.

DR. FRANKLIN sat behind the desk in his office, studying the lab report on Lee Miller. He was greatly relieved that the blood test had shown no traces of rabies virus. It would have been a terrible experience for the boy, as his father felt, to have undergone those treatments. The rest of the report corroborated the existence of an extremely large dose of toxic spider venom—species unknown; high white blood count; low acidity level. This, coupled with an obvious state of mild shock and exhaustion, would definitely account for the boy's present condition.

Still, he thought, even the largest dose of toxic venom should have already dissipated in the boy's system by now. What would account for the recurring symptoms of nausea, back pains and headaches?

After years of treating the boy for various childhood illnesses, he knew Lee Miller to have a tendency toward malingering, so he suspected that the boy was making somewhat more out of his present illness than was necessary.

Also, a vague memory came to him of an AMA bulletin he had read some months back—something about an expected outbreak of Russian flu throughout the seven western states. He went to his files, found it, sat down again to read it very carefully. The bulletin was put out as a precautionary measure by the U.S. Surgeon General's office and distributed through the AMA to physicians and medical organizations warning, among other things, about the possible outbreak of communicable diseases in given areas. This particular bulletin gave a description and details dealing with the possibility of an epidemic of Russian flu in the western quarter of the United States.

After reading the bulletin carefully he compared Lee Miller's symptoms to the predicted ones listed. It had to be the answer to the boy's persisting illness, he thought to himself. The symptoms matched perfectly. Lee Miller was very probably his first case of Russian flu.

He thought about the Millers insisting that he begin a series of highly technical, expensive and now entirely needless tests to discover what was wrong with their son. Now they were unnecessary; their son had developed a bad case of stomach flu. That was that.

Satisfied with his diagnosis of the Miller boy's condition, Dr. Franklin turned his attention to other, more important cases.

HARRY TURNED his car into the driveway and came to a screeching halt. He left the car, door ajar, motor still running, and ran up the steps to the porch and through the front door.

He had gotten the urgent phone call from his wife immediately after returning to his office after lunch telling him to come home, that something was wrong. He had made hasty and feeble excuses to the building contractors waiting to see him, told his secretary he would probably be gone for the day.

He closed the front door behind him, then stood for a moment to catch his breath. He heard movement down the hall and a pounding sound. "Jean," he called. "I'm home . . . what happened? Where's Lee?"

Jean came running down the hall to meet him. "Harry, Lee was terribly sick again this morning. He went into the bathroom to throw up. He fainted or something in there. I can't get the door open. Oh, Harry, I think he's dying in there."

Harry couldn't hide his annoyance. "Now don't talk foolish, Jean. He's not dying. Probably just sick and lying on the floor against the door."

"But I called to him, Harry. He doesn't answer me. . . ."

"Okay, okay, just calm down. I'll see if I can get the door open."

They hurried down the hall to the bathroom. Harry turned the doorknob; it turned easily. He put his shoulder to the door, slowly but steadily pushed. He could feel the weight against the other side of the door moving slowly. He kept on pushing.

Jean was pacing around behind him, wringing her hands.

Finally Harry got the door open far enough to look inside the bathroom. He leaned forward and stuck his head through the opening.

Lee was lying on his back, moving his head from side to side, mumbling to himself. The tile floor around the toilet and the front of his shirt were soaked with thick, brown vomit.

Harry pushed the door open a little further and squeezed in, closing it again behind him. He pulled his son up into a sitting position against the wall and wiped his face and hair with a towel. He wet a washcloth and wiped the boy's face. The cold cloth seemed to bring him to his senses. His eyes seemed to focus more clearly now.

"What the hell happened to you?" Harry asked, trying to keep the concern out of his voice.

"I . . . felt real sick, dad," Lee said between deep breaths. He shook his head to clear it. "I came in here because I was feeling bad. All of a sudden I got dizzy, really dizzy. I remember lying down on the floor to keep from falling. Then I got sick to my stomach again. I could hear you and mom out there but I couldn't get myself to move."

Jean's voice came to them from the hall. "What is it, Harry? Is he all right?"

"Yeah. He'll be okay, just a little dizzy." He turned back to his son. "Do you feel better now, Lee? Can you walk?"

Lee was struggling to his feet. "I think so, dad. I can . . . oh, god, I feel sick again." He bent forward and retched, this time into the toilet bowl.

When Lee felt a little better Harry helped him out of the bathroom and into his bed. He put a cold wet cloth across the boy's forehead. "If you don't feel good, or you need anything at all, just call us. We'll be in the living room," Harry said, and turned to leave.

"Dad," Lee said, "what's the matter with me? I've always thought I was in pretty good shape. Now I feel sick all the time, my stomach hurts, I have these awful headaches—"

"The doctor says you have the stomach flu . . ." He hesitated for a moment. "Lee . . . I know you're feeling bad because of the flu but . . . well, are you sure you're not pretending to be just a little sicker than you really are, to get out of going to school? . . ."

"I'm *not,* honest. I know I've done it before, but believe me . . . I *really* feel sick."

"Well, okay, but—"

"Dad, I'm not telling mom everything 'cause I don't want to worry her—"

"Okay, boy, okay, I believe you," his father said, smiling at his son. "Now, try to get some rest."

Harry walked into the living room. He was surprised to see that Jean was sitting on the sofa, a drink in her hand. She must have a real case of nerves, he thought. She almost never drinks liquor. . . . He looked at her with concern. "Jean, I want you to tell me exactly what the doctor said."

"He said he was sorry again about the argument the two of you had the last time he was here, that he doesn't often lose his temper like that—"

"I was right about no chance of rabies, wasn't I?"

"Yes, Harry. You were right . . . and so was Lee . . . there was a big dose of spider venom in Lee's system. But the doctor says that what happened to him lowered his resistance and made him more susceptible to a virus that caused the stomach flu. It was really bad this morning. He threw up in the doctor's office."

"How long is this stomach flu supposed to last?"

"The doctor said it's normally a twenty-four hour flu—"

"Twenty-four hours?" Harry said in disbelief. "The kid's been sick like this for five days now."

"The doctor says it could be hanging on like this because of his very low resistance and weakened condition. He doesn't feel any other tests or treatment are necessary, though. He gave me some medication for Lee. It should be over soon."

"I noticed the bandages came off his arm," Harry said. "It's looking pretty good."

"The doctor took them off this morning. His arm is almost completely healed. All he'll have are some small scars."

Harry jumped to his feet. "Goddamn it!" he said, heading for the door.

"What's the matter?" Jean asked, confused. "Where are you going?"

Harry grinned at her puzzled expression. "I was in such a hurry to get in the house, I left the damn car running."

They felt they could afford to laugh, and it felt good.

Chapter 3

BUT DURING the next week the laughter quickly stopped and Harry's nervous, irritable intake of Scotch markedly increased. He was eating himself up with worry over his boy, and, unlike his wife, buying nothing of the reassuring diagnosis of Dr. Franklin that it was all psychosomatic, in the boy's head. . . .

"Are you *serious?*" he said to Jean. "You have a boy lying in his bedroom, doubled over with terrible stomach pains. In the last two weeks he's lost thirty pounds. Thirty pounds! He's had headaches, back pains, and constant diarrhea. Have you taken a close look at his skin and eyes? They look jaundiced. And you honestly believe that it's all in his mind—that a little loving care and a new teddy bear will make everything all right?"

"In Dr. Franklin's opinion that *is* the only possible answer," Jean said calmly, as if she were explaining it to a child. "I talked with him today, he showed me documented cases so similar to this you wouldn't believe it. It seems this sort of thing is much more common than you think, especially with adolescents—"

She was interrupted by a scream from Lee's bedroom. It was the kind of tortured sound that might come from a terribly suffering animal. For just an instant Harry's and Jean's eyes met, then they were both on their feet, Harry's drink spilling on the carpet. Running down the hall, they reached Lee's bedroom and threw the door open.

Lee was thrashing wildly on the bed, both hands clutching at his stomach, fingernails digging into the flesh. His pajama bottoms and the entire lower half of the bedsheet were soaked with blood. It dripped down at one corner, forming a small pool on the carpet.

Harry rushed to the bed and tore the pajamas open. The boy's fingernails dug and clawed into the back of his hands as he did so.

"Call Dr. Franklin!" Harry shouted to Jean over his son's screaming. "Get an ambulance! We've got to get this boy to the hospital! Now, Jean! Move your ass, woman!"

Jean was still standing in the doorway in shock. She blinked her eyes once, as if she were just returning to reality, then turned on her heels and ran to the phone.

Lee was rolling and kicking less violently now, but still he screamed. A trickle of blood from biting his tongue ran from the corner of his mouth and down his neck.

With the pajamas torn away Harry could see that the

blood that soaked the bed was coming from the boy's rectum. It was now coming in a darker color, almost black.

Harry gripped his son's wrists and held them down, trying to stop the clawing fingers from doing any more damage. The tendons stood out like taut wires on the boy's wrists and neck as he writhed and struggled. Harry Miller was a powerful man but it still took every ounce of his strength to keep the boy's wrists locked within his grasp.

Minutes later the struggling ceased completely, and the boy's body relaxed. His breathing became shallow and labored, and there was a slight wheezing sound in his chest.

Slowly, Harry relaxed his grip and stepped back. A strange movement caught his eye and he leaned closer to look. The boy's stomach was rippling with little moving ridges, as if air bubbles were trying to escape.

Jean came hurrying back into the bedroom. "I couldn't reach the doctor, he's out on an emergency call, but the ambulance is on its way."

Harry straightened up abruptly. "Get out of here!" he shouted, making an almost threatening move toward her. "Get out of this room!"

"Harry," Jean said in a terrified voice, "what is it? What's happened to him?"

Harry could see the beginning of total hysteria on her face, her hands were shaking. "I don't know. Some kind of fit or spasm," he lied. "He's unconscious now. There's nothing we can do for him until the ambulance gets here."

Jean looked down at the bed, a look of horror on her face. "But, all that blood—"

"He injured himself," Harry said, forcing calmness into his voice. "It's nothing to worry about." He took a quick glance over his shoulder at his son's abdomen. The tissue rippled and jumped with activity. He prayed to God the ambulance would hurry.

"Come on, Jean," he suggested lightly, "let's have another drink, it'll calm us down." Before she could say anything more he'd turned her around and ushered her out of the bedroom, closing the door behind them. Slowly he guided her down the hall to the living room and placed her in a chair. He went to the bar and hurriedly mixed two drinks, then sat down, almost nonchalantly, on the arm of her chair as he handed her a glass. Within minutes the siren from the ambulance could be heard in the distance, growing louder every moment.

Harry had the front door open and was standing impatiently in the doorway as the ambulance came to a squealing stop. Two white-coated attendants moved quickly up the steps to the porch.

"This way, hurry," Harry called out, already moving toward the hall, Jean following closely behind.

Quickly they entered Lee's bedroom, then froze in numbing shock at the sight.

Their son was dead. He lay spreadeagled on the bed, his head hanging over the edge, his mouth wide open, his eyes glazed and staring. Across his face, in his hair, and down his neck onto his chest was a multitude of small, black, hairy spiders. They were everywhere. They crawled on the bed, across the carpet, even on the windowsill by the open window. Some were glistening wet, leaving little blood-red smears as they crawled across the boy's face and down onto the pillow. Some were obviously feeding on his blood.

Harry gripped Jean's hand; they stood in stunned silence, not comprehending what they saw. One of the ambulance attendants turned his head and vomited against the wall, the sound of it snapping the others out of their shocked trance.

"Spiders," the other attendant uttered, shaking his head in disbelief. "The kid's covered with goddamned *spiders.*"

"Th-they're crawling into his m-mouth," Jean mumbled, and began sobbing hysterically. She held tightly to Harry's arm to keep herself from fainting.

Harry Miller finally understood what had happened to his son. And why. "They're not crawling into his mouth," he said almost calmly. "All those little bastards are crawling *out* of his mouth. They're all coming from inside of him."

Jean was unable to comprehend anything; she had lost all control. "Kill them! My god, kill them!" she cried hysterically, and ran forward, trying to stamp on the spiders with her shoe, but they moved with surprising speed and she managed to squash only a few. The rest scattered in all directions, going under and in between the furniture.

Harry grabbed the night table standing by the bed, sending the lamp sitting on it crashing to the floor. Using the flat top face down, grabbing the legs in each hand, he smashed it down again and again on the carpet, killing the spiders as they dropped off the bed onto the floor. Soon there were no spiders on Lee's body or on the bed, and very few moving across the carpet.

Harry had managed to kill a lot of them, but it was as if the young spiders had a direction and purpose of their own. Most of them seemed to be following an unseen trail across the carpet, up to the open window, and out into the warm summer night.

Chapter 4

POLICE LIEUTENANT George McNeal moaned with discomfort as the car went over a hard bump. "Take it easy with the driving, Williams," he said sourly. "I'm miserable enough."

"Sorry, Lieutenant," Williams said as he guided the car up the winding street.

"This is the worst case of indigestion I've ever had," McNeal moaned, rubbing his huge belly gingerly and adjusting his heavy frame to a more comfortable position on the seat. "I've got to stop eating all that fast-food crap, or it's gonna kill me." He popped two more antacid

25

tablets into his mouth, making six within the last hour.

The entire day had gone badly for McNeal. With a heavy case load and a million things to do, he hadn't stopped for lunch, which gave him a headache. For dinner they stopped at a local McDonald's, where he had put away three Big Macs, two orders of fries and a shake. Now, at well past midnight, his headache hadn't gone away, he was dead tired, and had a heartburn that could kill an elephant. He shifted his weight on the seat again, and let out a resounding belch.

"Now, what's this crap about a kid being eaten by spiders?"

"That's the report I got," Williams stated. "Kid named Miller. Investigating officers said the boy was killed by spiders. Detectives don't know what the hell to make of it."

"How did it happen?" McNeal asked. "I mean, was he playing in the backyard? Hiking in the hills?"

"From what I got, he was in his bedroom—"

"In his bedroom? Why do I always get the good ones?"

McNeal and Williams arrived at the Miller house five minutes later. McNeal got on the radio. "This is One-L-Sixteen," he said into the hand mike. "Show us Code Six at 19327 Green Oak Drive—possible Three—nine-nine P.C."

After a moment the metallic female voice came through. "One-L-Sixteen, roger."

McNeal hung up the mike, slid to the edge of the seat, and with a great deal of effort hoisted himself out of the car.

Williams got out and came around the front of the car. "What the hell's a Three-Nine-Nine?" he inquired. "Never heard of it."

"Look it up in the goddamn book," McNeal told him.

"Maybe you'll learn something." Williams was an intelligent enough guy, and a damn good cop, McNeal thought, but he just didn't take it all seriously enough; he'd probably be a sergeant the rest of his life. To McNeal's way of thinking, there was no room in police work for clowning around. After eighteen years on the force, twelve spent in Homicide, he had seen death in almost every imaginable form and found damn little humor in any of it.

The front of the Miller house was choked with police cars and ambulances. McNeal barely squeezed past bumpers and fenders parked every which way.

"Why would anyone want to live on the edge of nowhere?" Williams asked, easily navigating through the clutter. He pointed off to his right. "Griffith Park begins right over there. It's nothing but bush-clogged hills and canyons for about the next five miles in any direction."

"Don't you know it's considered a luxury by the rich to move out of the horribly crowded congested city away from us common folks and then perch their asses high on top of a mountain somewhere. . . . Also, some folks just don't like neighbors." He stumbled on the first step leading up to the house and went down hard on his knees. "Shit!" He picked himself up and brushed off his knees.

"Would you like me to carry you, lieutenant?"

"Williams, would you like me to break your ass—"

"Okay, sorry. Did you hurt yourself?"

"No, goddamn it, I'm fine. Now shut up and let's go."

They walked the rest of the way up the steps to the porch in silence.

Inside the house was confusion. Uniformed and plainclothes officers were everywhere. After looking around briefly, McNeal located the sergeant in charge. Mrs. Miller, he said, was in bed, heavily sedated. Steven was going to college at Berkeley, lived on campus, came home sometimes on weekends. Harry Miller, the father, was talking to reporters, who seemed to have better sources of information than the police.

McNeal walked into the bedroom, where the medical examiner and his assistant were just finishing up, as were the crime lab photographers. McNeal lifted the blood-stained sheet and looked at the boy's body, already beginning to bloat and stiffen from the first effects of rigor mortis. He asked Dr. Simmons, the medical examiner, what killed him.

"He bled to death from the rectum," Simmons said flatly. "There's been extensive internal bleeding in the lower tract, probably the large intestine. Massive blood loss. An autopsy tomorrow morning should tell us more."

"But . . . they couldn't have caused all that damage," McNeal said, indicating the squashed bodies of the dead spiders covering the carpet. "Not from just a few spider bites."

"They didn't bite him, I didn't find a single mark or puncture on the boy's body."

"Then how—?"

"I don't know, that's one of the things I hope to find out during the autopsy."

"Send a copy of the report up to my office," McNeal said, and left the bedroom to talk to Mr. Miller, whom he separated from the cluster of grumbling reporters.

"Mr. Miller, I'm Lieutenant McNeal, Central Homicide. I'd like to go over what's happened here."

Harry Miller took a gulp of the Scotch he was holding, then gazed at McNeal through bleary eyes, his head bobbing slightly. "What the hell does homicide have to do with this? My son wasn't murdered."

"Any case of death other than from natural causes has to be investigated by homicide and a report filed,"

McNeal intoned. "If it turns out to be an accidental death it ends right there as far as homicide is concerned." He wrote the date, time, and Harry Miller's name at the top of the page in his notebook. "Now, if you'll just tell me—"

"I've already told the thing six times!" Harry Miller said, waving a hand in McNeal's face. "Why don't you people leave me the hell alone?"

"I know how you must feel," McNeal said in a low voice, but . . . you said that the spiders were inside your boy, and came out through his mouth. Do you really believe that?"

"I *saw* them moving inside him. What the hell else could I think?"

"But you didn't actually see them coming out, did you?"

"Lieutenant, I—"

"Tell me the truth, Miller. Did you have a lot to drink tonight?"

"If you're saying I was drunk—"

"No, it's—it's just that the whole thing doesn't seem too likely, does it?"

"I don't know. I only know what I saw." He closed his eyes and took a deep breath. "Lee was stung or bitten by a spider about two weeks ago, out on the desert. He got very sick and was in pain ever since. The doctor kept telling us that it was nothing, that it would pass. We believed him. I don't know how the spiders got inside him, or if they really were inside him. I only know I saw something, and that something—killed him." He gave a helpless shrug.

McNeal closed his notebook. "Well, I guess that'll do it for now," he said. "I'll be in touch with you, Mr. Miller, and I'm sorry. I really am."

McNeal left Harry Miller staring into his drink and collected Williams.

29

"I read Sergeant Gregory's report. Do you buy Miller's story?" Williams asked him when they were in the car and driving back to the police building.

"Hard to do," McNeal answered. "Sounds pretty damn farfetched to me. We'll have to wait and see what the autopsy shows." He settled back on the seat and closed his eyes against the pounding in his forehead. His stomach still burned like fire. "It's been a long crappy day," he said. "I'm glad it's over."

He wondered if his wife Doris would still be up. That would be nice, he decided. With the late hours he'd been working lately it seemed he hardly saw her anymore. Maybe she'd give him something to get rid of this rotten heartburn. He made a silent vow to himself to stay out of McDonald's.

Chapter 5

MCNEAL SLAPPED the morning newspaper down on his desk and sat down heavily in his swivel chair. He looked at the BOY, 15, KILLED BY SPIDERS headline, shook his head and turned himself around in the chair to look out of the window at the overcast day. A definite threat of rain. It always seemed to rain the first two weeks in March. He remembered, March 9—Karin's birthday. How old was she now? Twenty-three? Twenty-four? He honestly couldn't remember. He knew she was married a little over two years ago and was about to make him a grandfather. . . . He was sorry he'd missed the intimate closeness of a father-daughter relationship during her growing up, he just always seemed to be working, always busy, never home. Well, at least he wouldn't forget her birthday. He'd have to remember to pick up something for her, something special—

The telephone rang sharply. "McNeal, Homicide."

"This is Dr. Simmons. If you have a few minutes, lieutenant, can you come down to the morgue? There's something about the Miller boy's autopsy I want to show you. I'd better explain it in person, I've never seen anything like it."

McNeal always felt ill at ease when he had to go down to the morgue. As a matter of fact, he hated it. Everything was so overly clean, antiseptic and white—the whole atmosphere made him nervous, the atmosphere of death—nothing living belonged here.

Dr. Simmons came out of his office to meet him, then led him to a bank of refrigerated cubicles covering one wall of the large room. He examined the name tags on the cubicle doors, opened the one marked MILLER, L. and slid out a stainless steel table with a body on it. He removed a plastic sheet covering the body, adjusted the angle of a strong overhead light, picked up a surgeon's probe from a table beside him.

"I'll try not to get too technical," he said, pointing with the probe to an area in the open and spread abdomen of the body. "The digestive tract has already been removed —it has no bearing on the examination at this point. Now, these are the kidneys," pointing with the probe to the organs, each surgically sectioned. "Notice that the left kidney is about twice the size of the right one. Now, when I spread the incision, see those tiny, round, fibrous balls? They're what's left of spider eggs. Hundreds of them."

"But how is that possible?" McNeal said, stunned.

32

"Where did they come from? How the hell did they get in there?"

"I don't know," Simmons admitted, shrugging his shoulders. "But I *can* tell you what happened after they got there." Again he indicated an area with the probe. "To get into the kidneys they would have to have come through the bloodstream. How they got into the bloodstream, I could only guess. The kidneys act as a filter for the circulatory system, filtering out impurities and foreign matter from the blood. The eggs were trapped by the kidneys and there they stayed, like hundreds of tiny kidney stones, while the body figured out how to get rid of them. They were too large to pass through the urethra. It's amazing the blockage didn't cause uremia. Have you any idea how excruciatingly painful that must have been?"

"But according to the father's statement," McNeal said, "the boy was examined nine different times by their family doctor—complete with blood test and urinalysis. How could what you're saying go completely unnoticed?"

"Oh, it's possible—if those were the only tests performed. The spider eggs would have moved out of the bloodstream and into the kidneys rather quickly and so wouldn't have shown up in a blood test. Considering the nature of his symptoms, though, he should at least have been X-rayed and fluoroscoped in the lower digestive tract. In any case"—Simmons again indicated the kidney with his probe—"the spider eggs were trapped there, in perfect ninety-eight point six body temperature for however long the gestation period is for them—about two weeks, I would guess. Then they hatched, hundreds of them, in both kidneys."

Dr. Simmons paused, waiting for a question or some response from McNeal. He got none, so he went on.

33

"After hatching, the baby spiders fed on their victim's blood. Then, by using teeth or fangs or claws—I don't know very much about spiders, you can find out from an expert if you want to. I know some good men in the field. . . . Anyway, by using claws or teeth or whatever they have, they cut, chewed, or clawed their way out of the kidneys, and immediately attacked and fed on every organ in sight—especially a main artery called the iliac artery, and the large and small intestines. They completely severed the iliac artery, which caused the massive internal bleeding—the chief cause of the boy's death. Cutting and perforating the lining of the stomach and lining of the small intestine gave them access for escape —through the stomach, up the esophagus and out through the mouth." Dr. Simmons straightened up and looked at McNeal. "Any questions?" He was actually smiling.

"Are you kidding? You're goddamn right I have questions. *How* did the spiders—?"

"I've told you everything I can. I can give you the name of an entomologist at the University of California Medical Center. He's an expert an arachnology. He should be able to help."

Dr. Simmons went into his office and came back a moment later with a name and address written on a piece of paper, which he handed to McNeal.

"I'll also need a copy of the autopsy report and any photographs of the body you have," McNeal told him.

Simmons handed McNeal the report and a series of black-and-white photographs.

"Thanks again, doc," McNeal said, turned and walked down the hall to the elevator. As he reached the door he heard his name being called and turned around. Dr. Simmons was hurrying down the hall with a small plastic bag in his hand.

"Here, take these with you, they might help. They were the only ones left reasonably intact of the samples I collected in the bedroom."

In the plastic bag were two squashed spiderlings.

Chapter 6

MCNEAL ENTERED the science building, looked around the huge lobby at the impressive, colorful scientific displays. Everything was so changed. . . . It had been over twenty-five years since he had last been on the UCLA campus. This building, for example, had not existed back then; this once was grassy lawn on which he and his girlfriend—now his wife—would sit during warm summer afternoons and enjoy their lunch, and a little of what the kids now called making out. He was, he guessed, suffering a mild attack of nostalgia, but what the hell. . . . They were good days, they were in love, and after graduation and for that first year of marriage they were totally involved and happy in each other's world. . . . And then Karin was born, and two weeks later he entered the Los Angeles Police Academy for six months of training. After graduating from the Police Academy, he began working eleven- and twelve-hour shifts; it seemed he was never home, except to sleep. His wife didn't seem to miss him too much, spending most of her time with a new infant, but McNeal realized that somehow it had all changed . . . not badly, but changed. Well, it was never going to be the same, those days were gone. Why worry them to death . . . he had a good marriage, didn't he? What was so bad? . . .

He consulted a directory on the wall and discovered ENTOMOLOGY and ARACHNOLOGY under the general heading ZOOLOGY on the sixth floor. Why did it always have to be the sixth floor? He looked around for an elevator; he always used the elevator when possible. Hell, he was a man in his fifties, and overweight. Once, after going up three flights in a hurry, he'd damn near passed out. He located the elevator, then had to wait fifteen minutes for it to come down.

On the sixth floor, McNeal learned that Entomology and Arachnology were in the east wing of the building. He went down a long hall bordering classrooms to his right, then turned left. Finally the hall widened into a large foyer containing seven consecutively numbered classrooms and two science laboratories. On the wall between the classrooms, and taking up most of the available floor space, were large glass showcases containing every conceivable insect and spider. At the far end of the foyer were what looked like faculty offices, which was where McNeal was headed.

On the frosted-glass door of one of the offices was DR. HAROLD E. BENJAMIN, B.S., M.S., PH.D., CHAIRMAN OF THE

38

DEPARTMENT OF ZOOLOGY, ENTOMOLOGY, AND ARACH-
NOLOGY. The man McNeal was looking for. He knocked
softly on the door, waited a moment, then knocked
again, this time a little harder.

"Yes? What is it? Come in, come in."

The gray-haired man sitting behind the large oak desk
gave him a stiff, appraising look. McNeal figured him to
be in his early sixties.

"Dr. Benjamin? I'm Lieutenant McNeal, Homicide."
McNeal produced his badge. "I'd like to speak with you
for a few moments, if I may." He moved to the desk, then
sat down in an overstuffed leather chair without waiting
to be asked.

"Well, please make it brief, lieutenant. I have a faculty
meeting in fifteen minutes, then a staff meeting. I'm really quite busy." He began shuffling the papers in front
of him into a neat pile.

McNeal thought he was a pompous jerk, but if he knew
his spiders. . . . He opened his briefcase and handed Dr.
Benjamin the autopsy report and the photographs, then
spent the next few minutes giving him a brief account of
what had occurred. While he talked, Dr. Benjamin
skimmed through the report and glanced at the pictures,
showing little interest.

"All very interesting, lieutenant, but I hardly see what
I can do to help you."

"Well, for one thing, you can help explain how a mess
of spiders got inside a fifteen-year-old boy. To say the
least, you'll admit that's highly unusual."

"Unusual, yes, but not impossible. The boy may have
eaten something off the ground—a piece of cactus, for
example. It could have been any number of things, but
whatever it was, it contained fertilized spider eggs. The
human body makes an ideal recipient host. The warm
body temperature would provide a nearly perfect envi-

ronment for the gestation of this type of egg. There are many documented cases on record of just this sort of thing—"

"Maybe so," McNeal said, "but it still wouldn't explain the spider eggs being in the boy's bloodstream, would it? The medical examiner said beyond a doubt—"

"He is mistaken. There would be no possible way for the eggs to have entered the circulatory system."

"But the medical examiner—"

"Lieutenant, I am rather familiar with the characteristics and physical limitations of these creatures, and I assure you what this medical examiner of yours proposes is absurd. Now, if you'll excuse me . . ."

McNeal didn't budge. Instead he reached again into his briefcase. "Doctor, perhaps you could take a look at these." He produced the clear plastic bag containing the spiders and laid it on the desk.

Dr. Benjamin removed one of the specimens from the bag and examined it briefly under a powerful magnifying glass. "This specimen has been badly mutilated," he said, turning the spider over carefully in the palm of his hand. "I can tell you that it's an extremely young spiderling of the suborder Mygalomorphae, or common tarantula—a rather large one at that." He studied it a little closer. "It has an unusually large head, well-developed carapace."

"Anything else unusual about it?"

"I'd have to take these specimens into the laboratory and dissect them, and even that would probably do little or no good, considering how damaged they are."

"I'd appreciate it if you'd try," McNeal said. "Anything you could learn would be of help."

"I really haven't the time at the moment," Dr. Benjamin said, glancing at his watch. "If you would stop back later this afternoon, I'll see if I'm able to tell you more."

40

McNeal stood up. "Thank you, doctor. I really would appreciate that." He turned and left the office, closing the door behind him, and wishing it were legal to strangle pompous asses.

Dr. Benjamin took a moment to clean his glasses. He idly picked up the specimen again and looked at it through the magnifying glass. Ordinary mygalomorph, nothing particularly unique about it. Except, perhaps, its seemingly abnormal size, and the single-clawed structure on each of the legs. It was a shame it was so badly crushed. He would have liked to have been able to add it to his collection in the foyer showcase. Well, maybe he'd take a look later, but for now he dropped the spider back into the plastic bag, and put it, along with the autopsy report and photographs, into his top desk drawer.

He left his office and hurried down the hall to the faculty meeting room. He was late for an important meeting.

It HAD been a long time since McNeal had had the time to sit and eat a leisurely lunch. Usually he would only have time to grab a quick sandwich on the run. Today he had spent a whole hour and a half enjoying a full-course lunch. Afterward he'd taken a walk through the Wilshire Boulevard shopping district, looking in store windows and browsing in the shops. Now he was seated on a bench in a small park, people watching.

He idly noted a police car stop a lady motorist for some traffic infraction, watched with amused interest as the officer got out of the patrol car and sauntered, damn near swaggered, over to the woman's car. The way he walked, the knife-sharp creases in his trousers, the way his hat rode on his head at just the right angle to keep his eyes in shadow, and all the while an older, more experienced senior officer sitting in the driver's seat of

41

the patrol car carefully watching his every move, made McNeal smile. The young officer was obviously a rookie, everything about him said that he couldn't have been more than three or four months on the force. And McNeal could remember when he had looked and acted exactly like that—such a long, long time ago. . . .

After graduating from the Police Academy he'd been all fired up for a crime-fighting career; corny, maybe, but true. He'd spent most of the first two years on foot patrol in the East Los Angeles commercial district, checking padlocks and rattling doors in the warehouse district. His constant partner was a senior officer, by two years, named Bryson, and together they would doggedly cover their half-mile-square area of warehouses. To say the least, this was not what officer McNeal had had in mind, but he'd give it a full shot if that's what it took to get what he did want. Every evening at nine sharp he'd show up for his watch in a clean, starched, well-tailored uniform, and he and Bryson would go out on their boring patrol. He'd get off at seven the following morning. No trouble, no excitement, until the night of the break-in at the Finster Office Supply Company.

McNeal and Bryson had just finished the second round of their patrol, which was marked by a police call box on the intersecting corner, when they heard the sound of breaking glass. Bryson went to investigate, instructing McNeal to stay put by the call box. Bryson returned ten minutes later reporting that four suspects had broken into the Finster warehouse and were now loading crated office equipment into the back of a large panel truck. They called for police assistance, went inside the warehouse through the wide-open garage door with guns drawn and identified themselves as police officers, announcing that everyone was under arrest. But a fifth suspect was sitting behind the wheel in the panel truck, idling the engine. The suspect put the truck in gear and went speeding toward the two officers. Bryson managed to jump out of the way, but the truck's left front fender struck McNeal, sending him flying into a stack of packing crates. Bryson immediately got to his feet, and one of the suspects shot him twice in the stomach. Minutes later, when three more police cars arrived, they immediately called an ambulance for Bryson. It was found that McNeal had shot and killed two of the suspects, and had physically subdued the other three with the good use of his nightstick. He'd managed all this, moreover, while suffering a broken left wrist and a hairline skull fracture. Officer McNeal was awarded the Medal of Valor—something he was damn proud of to this day. Bryson recovered, and they'd been close friends ever since.

In those days he had been two hundred and twenty-five pounds of rock-hard muscle. Today—McNeal looked down at himself and shook his head sadly.

DR. BENJAMIN was busily trying to make a dent in the mound of papers piled up on his desk when McNeal returned to his office at three-thirty that afternoon.

"Well, doctor," McNeal asked, seating himself in the leather chair, "were you able to find anything out of the ordinary about those spiders?"

"Oh, lieutenant," Dr. Benjamin said, setting down the file he had been reading, "I've been so busy going over these student evaluations, I'd forgotten you were coming back this afternoon." He reached into his desk drawer and retrieved the autopsy report and photographs, being careful to bypass the plastic bag of spiders.

"Did you have time to dissect those spiders?" McNeal asked.

"I did examine the specimens," Dr. Benjamin answered, avoiding the actual question. "Except for some differences that wouldn't concern you in the least, I found them to be ordinary tarantulas. Nothing more. As I told you, the only explanation is that the boy ate the eggs."

McNeal stood up. "Well, doctor," he said, extending his hand, "looks like the end of the trail. I guess it's got to be accidental death. Thanks for your help." They shook hands, and McNeal gathered up his report and photographs, then left the office.

Walking down the hall toward the elevator, he forced himself to think about other, more important cases.

Dr. Benjamin sat behind his desk for a moment and thought briefly about what a shame it was for a boy to die like that. Then, picking up the file he had been reading, he too put the entire matter out of his mind.

Chapter 7

THE GRIFFITH Park area encompasses about twenty-five square miles of the Hollywood hills. In the park proper there are picnic and camping grounds, riding trails, and sports and recreational facilities. It is also the home of the Griffith Park Observatory and the Los Angeles County Zoo. Although all these facilities are located within the park they take up only a small part. Most of the Griffith Park area is a deserted wilderness of tangled brush and overgrown trees. It is abundant with small wild animals, including squirrels, gophers, and jackrabbits. Hardly a clump of trees or patch of brush that isn't

45

infested with holes and burrows of some type. Jackrabbits and gophers especially thrive here.

It was a warm, moonlit night. A colony of jackrabbits was feeding on the soft rich grass that grew abundantly around their burrows. It was a peaceful night—except for a slight breeze rustling gently through the trees. From time to time, one or two of the males would rear up on their hind legs, eyes wide, ears rotating like radar trying to sense any danger in the area. Satisfied that nothing was threatning them, they would relax and go back to grazing.

The grass began to move, and there came a slight rustling sound from the dry leaves under a grove of trees.

The entire colony froze.

The rustling grew steadily closer; now little black shadows were moving through the grass toward the rabbits.

The rabbit colony bolted, heading for the safety of their burrows. One by one they disappeared into the ground.

One bunny was not fast enough. The shadows swarmed over it, grabbing it with sharp claws and biting into it with fangs. For a few seconds it fought and struggled, then lay still—to be devoured, to have every ounce of its life's blood sucked from its body.

The spiders were on the move; they were hunting. They traveled and hunted as a colony—there were close to a thousand of them. They had grown considerably over the past six months since their escape from the Miller boy, and now averaged some three inches in length. They now attacked in a group—a predatory black mass of death.

They followed the rabbits into their burrows, swarming into the holes from all directions, trapping the rabbits, killing and feeding on them. They would take over the rabbits' burrows, the gosphers' burrows, any hole or cave or crag in the rocks they could find. They would make nests in which to lay their eggs, and they would multiply in numbers.

Chapter 8

THE WARM summer hung on longer than usual that year —until almost the middle of October. It had been an extremely stuffy summer, with temperatures in the low nineties, and almost no wind; the warm summer air just seemed to hang motionless, and it was hard to breathe.

Bobby Lembeck was glad the weather was cool today. Today was Saturday, his favorite day of the week. There was no school and he and his older brother Michael would always go on some sort of adventure.

Last Saturday they had snuck into an adult movie theater through an unlocked rear door and had seen two

X-rated movies. They were so afraid of getting caught they had spent most of the time hiding under the seats in the back of the theater and had not seen much of the show. What little Bobby did see he didn't fully understand, anyway. It seemed to be just a lot of people fighting on a bed with no clothes on. But Mike surely seemed to enjoy it.

Today they were doing something Bobby really liked. Today they were riding their bikes up to Griffith Park to go hiking. And if they were really lucky, maybe they'd even catch a gopher snake.

Bobby was glad when they reached the end of the winding blacktop road; his legs were getting cramped and tired from peddling the bike the last four miles up to this spot. They pulled their bikes off the road and into the tangled bushes to hide them. Bobby removed his pack and canteen from the carrier on the back of his bike. He strapped the pack on his back, then clipped the canteen on his belt.

"Are we gonna take our BB guns?" Bobby asked his older brother hopefully. "Just in case we meet up with wild Indians."

"No. We'll leave 'em," Mike answered with authority. "Anyhow, there ain't no wild Indians out there today. They're all off for the weekend, but we will take our knives and snakebite kits—just in case." He kept a straight, serious face.

"In case of what? There ain't no poisonous snakes up there. Are there?"

"Sure there are. Some of them get to be fifteen or twenty feet long. They could swallow a little kid like you whole."

"Gee—you're kidding . . . you ever seen one?"

"Sure. The last time I was up here hiking with the Boy

Scouts. It grabbed ahold of me and we fought for half an hour."

"Wow! What happened then?"

"Why, it killed me, of course, and ate me for dinner," and he put his arm around his brother's shoulders and tousled his hair.

They started off into the thick brush and up the side of a hill. The tall grass was still damp with the morning dew, wetting their boots and the cuffs of their pants. Mike was careful to keep the needle of his compass pointing north and made little identifying marks on the sides of trees with his knife as they went so they wouldn't get lost.

After hiking steadily for about two hours they stopped to rest and eat some sandwiches that Bobby was carrying in his pack. The water from their canteens tasted warm and metallic, but at least it was wet.

"Which way do you want to go now?" Bobby asked after they'd finished eating. He usually left decisions like that up to his big brother.

Mike looked around the area. "We're gonna climb up —there!" he announced, pointing to a steep grade ending in an overhanging cliff.

"Oh, I don't know," Bobby said doubtfully. "Why do you want to climb that, anyway?"

"Because it's there!" Mike announced dramatically, having heard or read someone say it about a mountain.

Climbing up the steep grade was harder than the boys had expected. They had to make their own footholds most of the way and grab tree branches to pull themselves up. The rough bark cut their hands, and a few times the small tree limbs broke loose in their grip and they almost fell.

While going around the side of a large boulder, the

small rocks and soft dirt gave way from beneath Bobby's boots and he tumbled backward, head over heels for some twenty feet down the steep hill. A tangle of thick brush finally stopped his fall, and he lay stunned.

Mike hurried quickly down to help his brother. "Bobby! Are you all right?" he shouted, finally reaching him. There was a touch of panic in his voice.

Bobby's shirt was badly torn, and both of his arms were scratched and bleeding. He got up into a sitting position and rubbed his stinging arms. "I'm okay . . . I guess," he said, looking at the blood smeared on his hands. "But, these sure sting."

"Can you walk?" Mike asked, still worried.

"Yeah, sure. I'm okay, honest." Bobby got shakily to his feet.

"Maybe we'd better quit and go home," Mike suggested, still looking at the bloody scratches on his brother's arms. "Mom would break my neck if I let anything happen—"

"Come on, Mike, I'm not a baby. So I fell down, so what? I can take it."

"Well . . . okay . . . if you're sure . . ."

They started back up the hill, this time going slower and being more careful. By this time the sun had climbed almost directly overhead and was beating down on their backs, making them sweat from the heat and effort.

As they neared some soft level ground, Bobby suddenly stopped and pointed. "Look, Mike—a cave!"

Mike dropped to his knees and looked into the jagged, dark hole. "Gee," he said. "I wonder how far in it goes?"

"Let's go in and find out," Bobby suggested bravely. Taking a flashlight from his pack, he aimed a beam of light into the cave.

"I don't know," Mike said. "I've heard of guys getting lost in places like that and never finding their way out."

"Come on, Mike," Bobby challenged. "Don't be a chicken." He got down on his hands and knees, then slowly started crawling into the cave. Mike hesitated for only a moment, then followed his brother in.

They crawled for about thirty yards, Bobby shining the flashlight ahead of them. Bobby started sneezing from the dust they were kicking up as they crawled. It was unusually cold and damp in the cave.

"Damn," Mike said, looking around at the walls of the cave. "What a creepy place. Look at all those spider webs. I'll bet we're the first people ever to come in here."

They heard a series of rustling, scraping noises coming from the space ahead of them. "Holy God," Mike whispered. "Come on, Bobby, let's get the hell *out* of here."

"Oh, Mike, come on, don't be afraid. It's only—" His flashlight illumined what was moving in the cave ahead of him. He let out a shriek and tried desperately to back up, banging into Mike right behind him.

They barely managed to turn themselves around in the narrow tunnel. Bobby dropped the flashlight and it went out, plunging them into an inky, chilling darkness.

The two boys crawled as fast as they could, but it was not fast enough. The crawling death coming swiftly up from behind caught them. They screamed until their throats were raw, and fought with every ounce of their strength. After a short while, their screaming and struggling stopped.

Police and Sheriff search and rescue units combed the Griffith Park area for three days, but the boys' bodies were never found.

BEING NOCTURNAL creatures, the spiders stayed in their burrows and caves during the day. Griffith Park was not used as a lovers' lane very often at this time of year, so

53

at night, when the spiders grouped and went out hunting, there was usually nobody around to see them. Except . . .

"Whatever makes you want to drive all the way up there?" Anne Rhudell asked disapprovingly. "It's awfully far up in the mountains, and I don't like this winding road. It makes me nervous."

Henry Rhudell drove quietly. He shifted the Rambler into low gear, maneuvering it around a hairpin curve, and smiled sweetly at his wife. She had gotten into the habit of complaining about everything the last few years, whether she really meant it or not. Maybe, just maybe, he thought, when they got there and she saw the old spot again she might remember how wonderful and exciting it had all once been. Maybe.

After being married for thirty-nine years, they were as comfortable with and as accustomed to each other as two people could be. Each was pretty much the other's whole life. Their children, grown and living lives of their own, came to visit only occasionally. They were content with just being together. But was content enough?

He knew she thought of herself as an old woman, but to him she was younger and more beautiful—and he loved her more now—than the day he'd married her. He wanted her to feel that way about herself.

They drove around the last curve and up to the crest of the hill, where the road ended. He pulled the car to the edge of the canyon, and turned the engine off. It was quiet and restful. Above them, a full moon set low in a sky filled with stars. Spread out in front of them were the lights of the entire city, like a grid map of winking lights and colored patterns.

"Oh, Henry, I *had* forgotten how lovely it was," Anne said after a moment. "And thank you for remembering this place." She moved closer to him.

"I've never forgotten it. I thought maybe you had." He put his arm around her and drew her closer to him.

"I love you, Henry," she whispered, kissing him on the cheek.

"And I love you too," he answered seriously. "I want you to *know* that."

"I do. . . . Do you remember the first time you brought me up here?"

"I most surely do," he said, leering at her, his hand moving down to her breast.

"You old fool," she admonished jokingly, slapping his hand away. "Get that out of your mind."

"Old fool, am I?" He grabbed for her again. "Well, if you'll just hold still I'll show you who's—"

A metallic scraping sound interrupted.

"What was that?" Anne asked nervously.

Henry put a finger to his lips, straining to locate the sound as it came again.

An instant later, the first of the spiders came clambering over the top of their hood. They sat in shocked silence for a few seconds, trying to comprehend what they saw. Anne instinctively pushed herself back against the seat, trying to get as far away as possible from the horror she saw in front of her. She sat stiffly, eyes staring.

Henry only mumbled, "Christ," and continued staring numbly through the windshield.

The spiders were advancing across the hood of the car, toward the windshield. Hundreds of them, as big as his hand. Henry could see little pinpoints of light as the spiders' eyes caught the moonlight. The closest spiders tested the windshield glass with their front legs, scratching at it. More were coming up the fenders of the car, their claws slipping on the smooth metal. Some slid off completely.

They could hear more scraping at the sides of the car

as the spiders tried to gain a foothold and climb up. The ground was now covered with spiders, and more were coming up out of the canyon in front of the car.

Some managed to climb up the side of the car; they were almost to the top of the door frame. Henry frantically rolled up the window. One huge spider rode up with it, its front legs hooked over the top of the glass. When the window reached the top of the channel, it severed the legs and the body of the spider dropped off.

With the windows rolled up, the spiders couldn't get in. They were safe.

Henry turned the ignition key and pumped madly at the accelerator pedal. The engine turned over, but wouldn't start; he had flooded the carburetor. Now, if the battery went dead . . . It took all of his willpower just to sit and watch the spiders milling around outside the car.

He waited a minute, then tried starting the car again, more slowly this time. The engine roared to life. He slapped the car into reverse, slammed his foot down on the accelerator. The car jerked backward, leaving a squashed trail where the tires cut a path through the blanket of spiders covering the ground. He whipped the steering wheel around, put the car into first, then slammed the accelerator again. The tires squealed in the dirt, sending up a cloud of dust behind them as they flew down the dirt road.

They had made it! Thank God, they had gotten away. He glanced at the speedometer, they were already doing sixty-five.

He looked over at Anne; mercifully, she had fainted. Her eyes were closed and her head was tilted back on the seat.

He realized too late that they were coming to a sharp curve. He slammed his foot on the brakes as he went into the curve, but the tires, slipping in the soft sand on the shoulder of the road, let go and they were sliding sideways. He quickly took Anne's hand in his as the left side of the car crashed through the wooden guardrail and it went hurtling out into space. As the car hit a boulder some fifty yards down the canyon the gas tank ruptured and exploded, and it careened and rolled the rest of the way down the steep, rocky hill, a bright ball of orange flames, until it came to rest on the floor of the canyon.

It took the firemen, complete with cranes and a tow-truck, six hours to pull the Rhudell car out of the canyon. All they found inside the car were charred bones.

The firemen couldn't figure out what could have caused the accident; after all, anyone with sense at all wouldn't be speeding on winding mountain roads like these, would they?

If they had looked about five hundred yards up the road, just out of the reach of the floodlights, they would have seen a thick, black, hairy blanket crossing the road.

IN THE cold winter months, the spiders went underground—to nest and mate and hibernate. They would not surface for the next four months. But, come March, when the weather warmed slightly, and the new generation of spiderlings had hatched . . .

Cheryl Hudson was worried. "If mom and dad knew I was coming up here camping with you instead of going to Judy's house, they'd break my neck," she said sullenly, looking at Jim. She didn't like sneaking off like this. She especially didn't like lying to her parents. They were always pretty cool with her, and they didn't deserve it.

"Don't worry, babe," Jim Baldwin said, grinning at her. He eased the station wagon slowly over a deep rut, then back onto the dirt road again. "We have it all nicely covered with Judy," he explained. "If your parents call, she'll make excuses for you. Your mom and dad will never know. Besides," he added confidently, "it's gonna be—great!"

She studied his handsome profile as he concentrated on driving over the sharply turning dirt road; nothing ever seemed to worry him. All the girls in their classes in high school were nuts over him, and he knew it. But she was the only girl he dated. Inwardly, she was proud of that but god, he thought he was hot stuff. Secretly, she admitted to herself, he was.

Jim pulled the station wagon off the dirt road and into a secluded grove of trees. "Well, here we are," he said, turning off the engine and getting out of the wagon. "You now have all the privacy you could ever ask for." He went around to the back of the wagon to open the tailgate.

"Where the hell are we?" Cheryl asked, looking around, bewildered.

"Oh, just a spot in Griffith Park that I . . . uh, heard about from some friends. You'll like it here. It's really nice."

"You've never been here before?" she asked suspiciously.

"Who, me? No, no, of course not. When would I come here?"

"Then how come—?" And thought better of it. No arguments, she told herself. Nothing to spoil their weekend together.

She helped Jim unload a large tent and other camping equipment from the back of the station wagon. They carried all the stuff to a clearing in the center of the grove of trees. After setting up the tent, they blew up the air mattress, then put the barbecue together. Within twenty minutes Cheryl had hamburgers and hot dogs sizzling on the grill.

By the time they had finished eating and had cleaned and put away the utensils the sun was just going down behind the hills in the west, casting long shadows among the trees. Jim lit a pair of Coleman lanterns. He set one lantern inside the tent on a small plastic table; the other he set on their picnic table outside.

"Well," Jim said, with an exaggerated yawning gesture, stretching his arms high over his head, "we might as well hit the sack." He grinned wickedly at her. "You ready for bed?"

"Yeah. I sure am tired," she answered, grinning right back at him. She wasn't really ready to go to bed with him yet, and didn't appreciate being rushed. She would have enjoyed sitting outside in the cool breeze of the evening, talking for a while. It really would have been nice and relaxing. But . . . she had come along, she could hardly back out now, and he did seem so eager. . . .

They entered the tent and pulled the flap down, closing it.

Cheryl laid out two pillows and a blanket on the air mattress, then, out of force of habit, turned her back to unbutton and remove her blouse. She unfastened the snap on her jeans and zipped them down. She had bought these jeans one size too small because they did wonders for her figure, but it was simply impossible to breathe in them. She kicked off her shoes, and with difficulty slid her pants down over her legs.

The two other times they had made love, both times had been on the rear seat of his station wagon. They had been hurried affairs, with uncomfortably bunched and rumpled clothes, quick, searching movements. And they had always been incomplete—at least for her. This was going to be different, she told herself.

She reached her hands behind her back to unhook her bra, and her fingers fumbled nervously with the clasp.

59

She felt flustered and embarrassed; her hands were shaking. She realized that she had never done anything quite like this before. Oh, she had played many games of squeeze and feel in the back seat of many cars with many boys, but she realized that she had never seen Jim, or any other boy, completely in the nude. Of course she had seen pictures and heard the stories the other girls told, but, except for seeing her little brother in the bath, she had never actually seen a male sex organ.

She glanced at Jim out of the corner of her eye, hoping he couldn't see her nervousness.

He had finished getting undressed and had gotten under the blanket. He lay with his hands behind his head watching her intently, his excitement evident by the rise in the blanket at his midsection.

She took a deep breath and carefully unhooked her bra, shrugging her shoulders and letting it fall to her feet. Hooking her thumbs in the waistband of her panties, she slid them slowly down and off. Then she turned to face him.

His eyes roamed slowly up and down her body, making her blush. His scrutiny made the nipples on her breasts hard and erect with excitement.

"Beautiful," he said softly. "You look just beautiful." Without taking his eyes off her, he pulled the blanket off himself.

She stared at him. His body was so hairy. And she was finally seeing his erect penis—it was huge! He was holding it in his hand as though it needed support. She started to giggle, then to laugh.

"What's so damn funny?" he asked indignantly, covering himself again.

"Nothing. Nothing at all," she answered, the tears rolling down her face from laughing. "But—" She started laughing all over again.

"I don't think it's funny," he said coldly.

She went over and lay down beside him on the soft air mattress, and started kissing his ear. That always made him feel better. She trailed the tip of her moist tongue from his earlobe, down along his jaw line, and onto his throat.

"Oh, baby," he whispered, his arms going around her, squashing her against his chest. He kissed her passionately on the mouth.

She responded, locking her arms tightly around his neck, and sending her tongue slithering between his teeth.

He maneuvered himself on top of her, and they began rolling and squirming in each other's arms, feeling, sensing, tasting each other. Kicking the blanket completely off them, he moved his hand down across her stomach and onto her soft, fleecy pubic mount, one finger probing the inner lips of her vagina.

She spread her legs wide to receive him.

He moved his hips in a long stroke and he was in her, then began moving his hips in a slow rhythm.

She let out a long moan, and lightly dug her fingernails into his back.

"Put your legs around my waist," he whispered.

"Ooh," she mumbled. "Just—like—this. This—is—wonderful. Now sloow—ooh—yes—ooh. OUCH!"

He looked at her, passion still clouding his eyes. "What do you mean—ouch?"

"Something's biting my leg!" she cried, pushing against his chest. "Get off! Hurry!"

He quickly rolled off her, and they looked to see what it was.

A large, hairy spider was sitting on the calf of her leg, its fangs embedded in her flesh.

"Oh, Jimmy—get it off! Pleaase!" She began shaking

61

her leg wildly, but the spider stayed on, digging its claws in even deeper.

Jim slapped with the palm of his hand, sending the spider flying. It hit the side of the tent and bounced to the ground, righting itself at once. Jim grabbed his shoe, and with two hard raps crushed it into oblivion.

"Goddamn," Jim said in amazement. "That's the biggest goddamn spider I ever saw. Cheryl, did you see the *size* of that bastard?" He looked at her face. "Ah, honey, don't cry." He took her in his arms and she did cry against his chest.

She was completely shaken. She hated spiders more than anything in the world. More than insects and snakes, or anything she could imagine. God, she thought, one was walking on her, actually bit her. "Jimmy, please,"—her face still against his shoulder—"let's pack up and get out of here. Please, Jimmy. I'm really scared." She shivered as she said it.

"Oh, come on, Cheryl," he said lightly, "don't ruin a whole weekend over one lousy spider." He kneeled down and examined the spider bite, wiping away a few drops of blood. "The bite's nothing to worry about. It's just a scratch."

"Well, I still want to leave," she said firmly. "Anyhow, it's starting to get windy outside. I can hear the trees and grass rustling. Come on, Jimmy. Let's go home."

Jim raised the flap and glanced outside the tent. The tree branches were standing still. The grass was moving a little, off on the other side of the clearing, but that certainly wasn't anything to worry about. "You don't need to be scared," he said, closing the flap again and returning to her. "I promise you, nothing is going to hurt you while I'm here. Now just relax. Okay?"

Cheryl was sitting on the air mattress with the blanket wrapped tightly around her, looking miserable. "I can't relax," she wailed. "That damn spider really scared me. Jimmy, I want to go home . . ."

He went over to where his clothes were piled on the ground, dug into one of the pockets of his pants and produced a hand-rolled cigarette, twisted at both ends. "I was going to save this for later, or maybe even tomorrow. But I think now is the time." He brought it over and showed it to her.

"Oh," she said, eyeing the joint of marijuana apprehensively. "I've smoked that stuff before. It was a big nothing."

"This stuff's really good," he assured her. "You probably just smoked it wrong. If you smoke it like a regular cigarette, you lose the whole effect." He kneeled down beside her and put a soothing arm around her shoulder. "Come on, Cheryl, have just one with me. It'll make you feel better."

"If I do, will you promise to pack up and get out of here?" she bargained. "This place really makes me nervous."

"Okay, sure, after we finish smoking this, we'll go." He put the joint between his lips. "I better show you how to do it right," he said, lighting the end. "All you do is take in a little smoke, then suck a lot of air into your lungs, and hold it for a while." He demonstrated.

"This smells funny," she said, sniffing the pale gray smoke. "Not like what I had before."

"It's pure Colombian," he said proudly, passing her the joint. "Here, try it."

She gingerly put the joint to her lips and took a short drag, then sucked in air the way she had seen him do. She held the smoke for a few seconds, then released it. "It doesn't taste very strong. Nothing's happening."

"Don't worry, it will." He took the joint back and took a long drag himself.

63

By her fifth drag Cheryl was in a state of euphoria. "Ooh, my arms feel like they're made of lead. I can't even hold them up." She giggled, handing the burning stub back to Jim. "I feel all limp inside."

"Mmm . . ." he said, sucking at the stub. "Here, there's one last drag in it. Be careful you don't burn your lips."

"No, you have it," she said, watching the flickering flame of the Coleman lantern, which seemed to have a hypnotic effect on her.

Jim took the last drag, then snubbed out the tiny butt in the dirt. "Feel better?" he asked, lying back on the mattress.

"Mmm, yeah," she answered, falling back on the mattress to join him. "Look at the shadows," she said, pointing an unsteady finger at the flickering shadows reflected from the top of the tent by the Coleman lantern. "That one looks like a doggie, and that one a snake. . . ."

Jim moved closer and began nuzzling her neck. She tilted her head to the side and closed her eyes. Physical sensations felt heightened, more than ever before. Everything felt so wonderful. . . .

He moved his lips down her throat to her breasts, trapped an erect nipple gently between his teeth. She moaned with pleasure as his lips toyed and sucked at her breast. She had never experienced such intense pleasure before. She gave herself over to it completely, allowed herself to be engulfed in sensation.

He moved slowly down her body, trailing his tongue across her ribs and belly until he reached her soft, curly mound. She spread her legs wide and curled her fingers in his hair as his face sank between her legs, his tongue gently penetrating the lips of her vagina.

They were both far too engrossed in each other to notice when first one, then two, then fifteen, then a wave of thousands of large black spiders came out of the grass and moved quickly across the clearing—toward their tent.

The spiders poured through the front flap of the tent and swarmed over them. With a scream of pain, Jim rolled off Cheryl and onto his back, spiders clawing and biting at his arms and legs. More came, covering his chest and stomach. Rolling and flailing his arms and legs wildly, he hit the table, sending the Coleman lantern crashing to the ground. It shattered, splashing ignited kerosene everywhere. A mass of spiders went up in flames, along with his hair and the entire back side of the tent. He continued rolling and screaming, swinging his arms and legs, now completely encrusted with spiders.

Cheryl rolled off the mattress, screaming. She, too, was completely covered with the huge, vicious spiders; they were in her hair, on her chest and stomach, clinging to her arms and legs; clawing and biting every part of her body. It was like having millions of razor-sharp little knives sticking into and gouging her flesh, all at the same time. She struggled to get to her feet, blindly staggered out of the tent.

Outside, her legs gave way, slipping on the moving bodies underfoot, and she fell backward, crushing dozens of spiders under her. It was getting more and more difficult to move her arms and legs; it was as if she had lost all control of them. Her limbs no longer responded to signals sent from her brain. She didn't dare scream anymore. They were clinging to her face. If she screamed they would crawl into her mouth. . . .

Agonizing minutes passed as she lay motionless in the midst of the moving, swarming bodies. She couldn't move her body at all now. It was as if she were completely paralyzed—but, oh God, she could feel! She could feel the fangs digging in and taking hold, the tiny, sharp claws ripping and tearing at her flesh. Her body was alive with excruciating, intolerable pain. What was left of her eyelids were swollen shut; her eyeballs burned terribly. She could feel the creatures moving and biting and tearing at her; she knew what they were doing to her, but it was as if her mind was a prisoner inside a completely useless and pain-destroyed body. She could hear them; hear the horrible sucking sounds they made; knew they were feeding—on her!

Gradually, her fingers and toes grew numb, then her arms and legs. The numbness seemed to move slowly from her outer extremities inward, toward the very center of her being. Finally, her entire body was dead—only her tortured mind was still alive.

The last rational thought Cheryl ever had was: Please, God, let it end.

Chapter 9

LIEUTENANT MCNEAL leaned against a tree, trying to catch his breath. He removed his coat and loosened his tie. His shirt was wringing wet with perspiration, it stuck to his back and chest. He unbuttoned his collar, mopped his face and neck with his handkerchief. The short walk up the dirt road to the campsite was too much for him; he was just too fat to go hiking around in the Griffith Park hills. He silently vowed to go on a strict diet.

He had heard the report come in over his radio while he was driving to his office that morning. "Any supervisor," the dispatcher had said. "Two dead bodies discovered by hikers in Griffith Park area." He had gotten curious and had detoured to answer the call. Now he was sorry he had ever bothered coming up here. Hiking was for Boy Scouts.

After a few moments his overtaxed heart quit banging in his chest, his pulse slowed, and his breathing returned to normal. He gave himself another minute of deep breathing, then continued up the dirt trail to the clearing. He bypassed the confusion of officers and lab men, all busily combing the campsite area and taking pictures and went directly over to where an SID man he knew who was standing and talking to a uniformed sergeant.

"Morning, Jefferson," McNeal said. "What's the story?"

"Good morning, lieutenant," Jefferson answered cheerfully. "What happened to you? You look like you ran a race and lost."

"Can the jokes," McNeal said, giving him a sour look.

"Okay, been a fire in the tent over there." Jefferson pointed to a half-burned tent, scorched table and a mass of melted rubber. "Two dead—boy and girl. The ME figures they've been dead about seventy-two hours."

"If the bodies were discovered by hikers this morning, who reported the fire?" McNeal asked.

"Nobody."

"How come the fire wasn't sighted by the Ranger lookout station? They couldn't have missed a fire at night."

"On account of the new fire-resistant chemicals and fabric these tents are made of these days. . . . There was an initial flare-up, caused, we figure, by an overturned lantern, and then the flames went out quickly. The tent just sort of smoldered and melted for about the next six hours without being noticed."

"If the fire burned that slowly, how the hell did those kids get burned to death?"

"They weren't burned to death. At least the ME doesn't think so. Not by the looks of them anyway. Those bodies are the damnedest things you ever saw."

"What do you mean?"

"Come over here, lieutenant. Take a look."

They went over to where plastic sheets covered two bodies on the ground. Jefferson pulled back one of the sheets; they both stared down at the body.

The first thing that hit McNeal was the suffocating, nauseating odor. An involuntary gasp escaped his lips. "Good Lord," he said, fighting to keep down the revulsion, "how long did you say they've been dead?"

"Dr. Simmons was out here about an hour ago. He estimates around seventy-two hours." Jefferson backed up a few feet. "He said that if you showed up he knew you'd be especially interested in this one."

McNeal put his handkerchief over his nose and mouth, got down on one knee to get a better look. Under anywhere near normal conditions decomposition of a human body took a good deal of time. . . . McNeal couldn't believe that *this* could have happened in just three days.

The body was obviously female, but what had happened to it? It was completely deflated. The skin was stretched tightly over bones and muscles, giving it a leathery, mummified look. The entire body was a purple-black color, and every inch of tissue was covered with tiny cuts and deep lacerations. The lips were drawn back over the teeth in a silent scream, and the eyes protruded from the head, sightlessly staring. Rigor mortis had bent the legs at the waist, giving the entire body a strange, contorted look. All around the area and under the body were large, dead spiders, curled and dried in the sun.

"Oh, I almost forgot," Jefferson said, reaching into his coat pocket. "Dr. Simmons left you a copy of his notes.

69

He said you'd want to see them." He handed the papers to McNeal.

McNeal read through them quickly; he couldn't believe what he read: complete loss of blood from the body; total loss of spinal fluid; total loss of pancreatic fluid; complete dehydration of the body. Something had sucked every ounce of fluid from both bodies.

"What do you suppose killed her, lieutenant? And did . . . *that* to her," Jefferson asked, shaking his head. "And what the hell killed all those spiders?"

Suddenly it all seemed very clear to McNeal. Too clear. "She killed those spiders . . . fighting for her life," he said, almost to himself. He glanced once more around the campsite. "I've got to get back to the city. Come on, Jefferson."

"Why? What do you need me for?"

"I'm going to be up to my ass digging through the files. I'm going to need help."

"What happened to Williams? Didn't he come with you? I thought the two of you were such buddies."

"He had personal business to attend to. Something about his son being sick. Now, come on, will you help me, or not?" Without waiting for an answer, he took Jefferson's arm and led him down the trail to where the car was parked.

McNeal rapped lightly on the frosted glass door to the captain's office. After a moment he heard a muffled, "Come in," entered the office, arms loaded with files and reports, and set them down on the desk in front of the captain.

He and Jefferson had spent the rest of that morning and half the afternoon in Missing Persons and Homicide going through and selecting reports and files that McNeal thought important or related to what he suspected was happening in Griffith Park. In his mind, it was pretty conclusive now.

Captain Bryson looked up from a report. "George, how are you? What have you got there?"

"Captain, I want you to look at these," McNeal said, unable to keep the excitement out of his voice. "We have something going on in the Griffith Park area, and if we don't do something about it, and fast—"

"Okay, take it easy, George. Slow down. And stop with that captain crap. The name's always been, Frank, you know that. Now what's this all about?"

McNeal took a deep breath. "All right," he said, starting again more slowly. "About a year ago I investigated a homicide—a young boy named Miller. The kid was killed somehow by a lot of spiders." He handed Bryson the report on Miller. "Since that time we've gotten report after report of missing persons or unexplained deaths—all in the Griffith Park area." He picked up a handful of files. "Look at these . . . two boys, Robert and Michael Lembeck, lost in the hills while hiking—in the Griffith Park area!" He picked up another report. "Henry and Anne Rhudell, burned to death in an automobile accident, after speeding—speeding, mind you—down a dangerous mountain road—Griffith Park area! John Finley, jogging in the Griffith Park area, disappears. Here's another one. Sheriffs search for missing Boy Scouts—*same* area. I have seventeen such reports—seventeen of them, all in the same area. Now, this morning they discovered a young couple that went camping three nights ago. You would have to see their bodies with your own eyes to believe what—*something* did to them. And all around the campsite area were huge dead spiders—and I mean gigantic. Stretched out, some of those spiders measured six to eight inches, leg to leg. Here's the report I just got on that. Look at it. I think we've got a real

71

nightmare out there." McNeal handed the newest report to Bryson.

Bryson skimmed over the report, then looked at McNeal. "You figure these spiders attacked the Miller boy—a year ago?"

"No! The Miller house is on the outskirts of the park area. I think the Miller boy brought the spiders into the Griffith Park area. How or why, I don't know. He brought them in from the desert. Read the full report, you'll see what I mean."

"Are you sure, it could all be just a—"

"Captain, I just finished talking to the forestry service in that area. There hasn't been a single animal seen in that area for over four months. No birds, no rabbits. Nothing. Something either ate them all, or scared them away."

Bryson eyed the stack of reports in front of him. "I'd like to go over these myself, then I'll assign a few men to help you in your investigation."

"There isn't time, and it'll take more than a couple of men."

"What do you suggest?"

"Close Griffith Park."

"Close the park? George, do you realize what—?"

"Captain, we can't let people into that area until we know exactly what we're up against. It has to be done, you can see that."

"I suppose you're right, but I've got to clear it higher up. Meantime you contact the sheriff's department and the highway patrol and see what you can do about borrowing some men."

"All right, I'll get on it." McNeal turned to leave.

"George . . ." Bryson was looking at him. "Very damn soon we're both going to be in this thing up to our ass. I hope you're right."

"I am," McNeal said firmly, and closed the door behind him. He went down the hall to his office, sat down heavily in the chair behind his desk. He felt good that Bryson was backing him up in this, but then, Bryson was the kind of man you could always count on. He could name more than one time when Bryson had gone way out on a limb strictly on his say-so. Bryson was now one of the best friends he had, professionally and socially; they'd known each other a long time. It hadn't always been that way. A few years back, when the promotion for captain was available, they'd both taken the examination and Bryson had beaten his score by just two points. Bryson had gotten the promotion to captain, and McNeal had resented it . . . until he'd finally come to realize that it wasn't, shouldn't be, a personal thing, and had adjusted. . . . He picked up the phone, at the same time thumbing through his telephone directory, then thought the hell with it and dialed the switchboard to get him the highway patrol.

LATER THAT afternoon Bryson gave him the bad news. The mayor had refused to close the Griffith Park area. It was the height of the tourist season, he was worried about the city's image, and the chief of police fell over backward to agree with His Honor all the way. It was, after all, an election year. The chief had his eye on a city council seat, hopefully with Mayor Bradshaw's support, for which he would kiss ass until the ballots were counted. "No action will be taken in this matter until more conclusive evidence is presented," was the chief's order to Bryson.

"More evidence!" McNeal shouted. "More bodies, he means."

"Look, George, you come up with anything tangible that I can use—not just theories—and I'll close that god-

damn park in one hour. On my own authority, if necessary. But give me something."

"Don't worry, captain. I will."

Which was also what he was afraid of.

Chapter 10

THE NIGHT was bitter cold. The kind of cold that could get inside you, chill the marrow of your bones. John Hennessey pulled the fur collar of his uniform jacket up around the back of his neck and lit another cigarette from the butt of the one he had just finished. He never could figure out how it could be eighty-five degrees and sunny during the day and so goddamn cold and damp at night. He pressed the little button on the side of his watch. The dial lit up the numerals: 3:16 A.M. The early morning dampness was just beginning to set in, making the lawn soggy with dew and causing his shoes to leave wet footprints as he walked. He shoved his hands deep into the furlined pockets of his jacket and continued down the asphalt trail toward the security building.

Except for the chilling coldness of some of the nights, being the senior security guard at the Los Angeles County Zoo wasn't a bad job at all. He punched in at eight P.M. every night, held a short meeting in the security building, assigned the seven other officers their roving patrols. Then he spent the rest of the night checking locks and in general making sure everything was secure and in order.

After retiring from the Marine Corps on a major's full retirement pay, he still needed to supplement his income. So he had taken this—and he enjoyed it. There never seemed to be any trouble, and he had always liked animals.

He unlocked the door to the security guard's facility room and went inside. He took the pot of steaming coffee from the hot plate by the sink, poured himself a large cup. While the coffee was cooling, he checked the time cards, which recorded each tour the officers made through the park, then punched his own into the time clock. It seemed like a particularly long night—the hours were dragging by. He couldn't wait until six o'clock when he was finally off.

At three-thirty A.M., he drank his coffee down in two long gulps, dug a fresh pack of cigarettes out of his desk drawer and left the security office to begin his fourth tour.

He followed the asphalt path up through the area of compounds called Africa, continued along the winding paved path toward the north end of the zoo. He would turn left, as his particular tour led him down another road to head back. The entire route usually took him about forty-five minutes.

He felt a little tense tonight. Nothing he could put his finger on, just a feeling on the back of his neck. Like someone was watching him. Unconsciously he quickened his step, and a few times actually caught himself glancing behind him. But the animals seemed to feel it too . . . they were restless, moving nervously around in their enclosures, making low noises among themselves. They were really on edge.

The only lights left on at night were at road intersections and at approximately every hundred yards along the paths, giving the entire area a half-lit, shadowy look. The same trees and shrubs that decorated the park so beautifully during the day at night took on an ominous look. It was certainly not a place for somebody with a vivid imagination; the noises and the shadows seemed to close in on you.

Hennessey reached for the two-way communicator hooked on his belt, pressed the side button. "Daniels—you read me?"

There was a crackle of static, then: "Yeah, Hennessey, Daniels here, where you at?"

"In the quad, by the snake house. How are things out your way?"

"Animals seem kind of spooked tonight. One of the big cats jumped at the fence—scared the livin' shit outa me."

"I know what you mean, same here. Well, make another tour around the north perimeter, and I'll see you around the European compound in, say, ten minutes. And make sure you smile and show plenty of teeth so I'll be able to see you." A small joke between them, which Daniels didn't seem to resent from Hennessey, though he damn well would have from another white man.

Hennessey contacted the other six guards, each patrolling a different segment of the zoo. They all gave him

77

about the same response—that everything was quiet and no sign of trouble, but the animals were jittery and nervous. He clipped the communicator back on his belt, continued up the road toward the North American compound, where he stopped long enough to light another cigarette, checked his watch again: 4:02.

As he entered the North American compound he heard a crunching noise behind him. He turned quickly around, his hand instinctively going to his revolver.

He listened. Silence. The trees were swaying a little in the early morning breeze, but other than that he could see or hear nothing.

What the hell was wrong with him tonight, he thought, holstering his gun again. Whatever the jumpy feeling was, it certainly was catching. He made up his mind to cool it, just take it easy.

Grrrr.

That noise was real. Hennessey looked around. It had come from off to his right—that group of cages there.

Grrrr. The low growl came again.

He entered the canine compound, walked quickly in the direction from which he thought the growl had come. He stopped in front of one of the cages, staring.

A large Alaskan timber wolf was backed into the corner of its cage. The hair from the tip of the wolf's nose, along the back of its neck and down the center of its back was standing straight up in either fear or aggression; even the hair on its tail bristled. The wolf's eyes were wide and glaring, its ears were back and its teeth were bared.

Hennessey stood transfixed. What the hell could frighten a two hundred pound timber wolf like that? Then he noticed that the wolf's eyes weren't on him, but on something behind him. He turned to look.

A huge black shadow was moving down the side of the

hill a short distance away. It covered the entire top of the hill, and half the way down. It must have stretched for a quarter of a mile—and it was moving, moving toward the zoo, making a rustling, crunching sound like a billion tiny feet moving through the grass and leaves.

It drew closer. Now it was at the chain-link fence on the outskirts of the zoo, and moving under it. Hennessey could make out individual shapes now; he could see what they were!

After being in this world for fifty-odd years and spending twenty of those years in the service and traveling all over the world, Hennessey had always thought he had seen it all. Now, after seeing what was creeping quickly toward him, getting closer every second, he dropped the flashlight he was carrying, turned on his heels, and ran in blind terror. He didn't look back; he didn't want to look back—he just ran. Off to his left he heard a series of six pistol shots, then a scream. He ran. He heard what he was sure were the dying screams and snorting bellows from the animals near the outskirts of the zoo. He could vividly imagine what was happening to them, even knew which animals they were. Still he ran. He heard more gunshots, followed by a human scream, then another as he ran through the darkness. His communicator began buzzing on his hip; he ignored it. He ignored the howling and bellowing of the animals around him. He ignored everything, with only one driving thought in his mind— to get away from the horror behind him.

Coming down the hill toward the administration buildings he left the path and cut across an expanse of soggy lawn, still running like hell. His shoes slipped on the wet grass and he went skidding and sliding on his stomach and hands for a short distance before smacking into a rubbish container and a bench. He picked himself up and immediately began running again—but limping slightly,

79

the entire front of his uniform dripping wet.

He reached the door to the security room still on a dead run, his hand frantically searching his pocket for the keys. He found them as he reached the door and pulled them out. He stood for a few seconds staring dully at a ring of about fifteen keys. Goddamn it—which key was it? He couldn't remember. He quickly started trying key after key. The fourth one fit and turned the lock. He threw the door open and rushed inside, slamming and bolting it behind him.

On the wall was the alarm switchboard. He threw all four switches simultaneously, a procedure reserved only for catastrophes like an earthquake or tidal wave. It put in an alarm to his security headquarters, three different fire departments and the four police precincts surrounding the zoo.

Hands shaking, he went to the cabinet under the sink and came up with a bottle of bourbon whiskey he had hidden there. He took three long pulls from the bottle, and felt the liquor immediately warm his insides and begin to calm his nerves.

He got on the telephone and warned the different departments about what they were facing. His story was met with ridicule, doubt—". . . if this is your idea of a joke—" to ". . . why don't you go sleep it off?"

The spiders were moving through the zoo, swarming over and covering everything in their path. They were attacking and killing every living thing in their way. Some would stay to feed while the mass pushed forward. The night was filled with the horrible sounds of death as the animals, trapped in cages and enclosures, tried to fight back but in the end fell before the unstoppable murderous wave of death.

Hennessey hung up the phone after talking to Emergency Riot Control. He had just lit another cigarette

80

when he heard a frantic banging on the door. He turned to look.

Daniels was banging with both fists, at the same time glancing behind him. His shirt was covered with blood, his arms were cut and bleeding. His normally brown skin was an ashen-gray color, and there was a nasty gash on his right cheek.

"Hennessey! Come on, man, open the door!" he shouted, glancing in terror over his shoulder. "Them motherfuckers are comin' right behind me!"

Hennessey jumped to his feet and took three quick steps toward the door, then stopped. He couldn't open the door. He couldn't take a chance of letting . . . *them* in.

Daniels looked behind him again. When he turned back, there was sheer panic on his face. "Come *on,* man —open the fuckin' door, *hurry!*"

Hennessey could only stare at him.

"Hennessey, f'god's sake, *please* . . ." There were tears coming down his face. He frantically beat on the door with the butt of his gun, but the reinforced shatterproof glass wouldn't break.

Hennessey stood fixed to the spot, staring at him.

"Hennessey! You son of a—" And then they were all over him, each spider fighting with claws and fangs for an exposed inch of flesh. Daniels beat at his face with both hands, desperately trying to keep them out of his eyes. A few dropped off, immediately to be replaced by others. Within seconds Daniels was no longer Daniels— he was a mass of hairy, squirming bodies, vaguely in the shape of a man.

As Hennessey watched, Daniels' body stiffened and twitched, then seemed to deflate within itself—like letting a small amount of air out of a balloon. Then it sagged slowly to the ground.

Hennessey's mind was numbed. He had to do it, he told himself. Otherwise they'd both have been dead. Wouldn't they? . . .

Outside, the ground was completely covered with a moving carpet of black, hairy bodies. Some of the spiders tried to climb the window; they slid off. Hennessey watched them silently for a few minutes. They could see him, he was sure of it, by the way they moved frantically toward the window as he walked by.

He went back to his desk, sat down heavily in the chair. They were outside, he was inside. He meant to keep it that way. He reached for the bottle of whiskey and took a long, shuddering drink.

Chapter 11

MCNEAL WAS in a deep sleep. He lay on his back with his hands folded across his chest, his body completely un-moving—his most comfortable sleeping position. He resembled a huge dead whale. The only indication that he was not dead was the snoring sounds that rever-berated from his wide-open mouth.

After leaving Bryson's office that afternoon he had carefully reread every one of the reports. Finding noth-ing new or useful, he had then driven out immediately to the area immediately surrounding Griffith Park and talked with the local residents. They had complained about every kind of disturbance imaginable, but not the kind he wanted to hear. When he finally had gotten home about eleven-thirty that night he had been too tired to eat dinner and had just taken a hot shower and fallen into bed. . . .

The telephone rang five times before he was sufficiently awake to answer it. He reached for the phone, his mind still dull with sleep. "Hello. Williams? Why the hell are you calling me at"—he switched on the bedside table lamp and looked at the clock—"quarter to goddamn five in the morning? You'd better have a good reason or so help me I'll have you . . . what? What! The zoo! Christ, yeah, okay, pick me up in ten." He cradled the phone and got out of bed. He stumbled into the bathroom and splashed cold water in his face, then looked at himself in the mirror, feeling the rough stubble on his chin with his hand. He looked like hell, the hell with it. . . . He put on the same suit he had worn the day before. Why put on a clean suit for this?

His wife stirred in bed, then sat up. "George, you're not going out again," she said, looking at him with genuine concern. "You just got home—"

"Something bad has happened," he said, tying his shoes.

"Where?"

"The zoo. That was Williams on the phone."

"But look at you. You've got to get some sleep or you'll—"

"I've got to go, Doris. Be back early if I can." He slipped his gun into its shoulder holster, put his coat on.

"George," she said softly. She reached out and lightly touched his arm. "Be careful?"

"I will," he answered. He leaned over and kissed her on the cheek. "Now go back to sleep. I'll be okay. Bet on it." He turned off the bedroom light and quietly left the house.

Spiders attacking the zoo, he thought. Good god! But that would mean even if they'd been able to close the park area they'd have been too late. If what Williams had said was true, there were millions of them now . . . how the hell did something like this get started? . . . Could it really have all begun with that business with the Miller boy? Could he be at least partly responsible for not investigating it more completely at the time? But that guy, Dr. Benjamin, had said he'd dissected and examined the specimens and found nothing unusual about them. He decided to have a long talk with Dr. Benjamin.

As he reached the curb in front of his house Williams came screeching around the corner and pulled up in front of McNeal, who wordlessly got in. They sped down the Ventura Freeway, then connected with the Golden State Freeway. Williams moved over to the extreme righthand lane, preparing to exit on Zoo Drive.

"I don't really know what the big deal is," Williams said, shaking his head. "There may be a lot of them, but spiders are spiders. You step on a spider—no more spiders. Right?"

"Wrong. You haven't seen these spiders. If you try to step on these babies they'll tear your leg off and beat you to death with it."

"Come on, lieutenant—"

"Believe me," McNeal said. "They've already killed a couple of dozen people—that we know of."

"It sounds impossible," Williams said, still skeptical.

Chaos prevailed at the zoo. Police and firemen were running in every direction, like ants on a hot day. Everybody was shouting orders at everyone else and nobody seemed to know what the hell to do. The police had nothing that could stop or even deter the advancing army of spiders. The only piece of equipment remotely useful was the fire department's high pressure hoses, but even these were only good for clearing a path through the spiders. As soon as the high pressure stream hit the spiders they would immediately curl into a tight ball and ride with the stream until it petered out, then right themselves and begin traveling again in the direction they were originally going.

McNeal and Williams parked in the middle of the road, as close as it seemed they could get to the zoo. It was impossible to park any closer because of the huge jumble of police cars and fire trucks. High pressure fire hoses snaked along the ground, spread to their maximum length and crisscrossing each other in a hundred different directions. To make matters worse the television news services had already arrived in large mobile vans. At the moment technicians were busily setting up the mobile television cameras at various points around the front of the zoo. Reporters with hand-held microphones were trying to interview anyone who would talk to them, but accomplishing nothing more than adding to the awful confusion.

"The news services monitor the police and fire bands," Williams said as they passed one of the mobile vans. "That's how they know so fast what's happening and where. Do you know, they can get a big unit like this moving in four minutes flat?"

"That's wonderful," McNeal said, and walked away, leaving Williams standing and looking at the television truck.

As McNeal approached the front of the zoo he saw some police officers cutting large holes with oversized bolt cutters in the chain-link fence surrounding the main

gate, others setting up floodlights to illuminate the area. Bryson stood on the rim of a large fountain at the main entrance to the zoo that shot water sixty feet into the air, then spilled it over four cement steps, giving them a waterfall effect. The water came to rest in a deep pool, complete with lilies floating in it. Bryson, shouting orders, saw McNeal approaching. "George, don't give me any 'I told you so' crap and help me get these idiots organized."

"Any casualties?" McNeal asked.

"Eight of our people injured, mostly from falling over something in the confusion. I talked to a security officer named Hennessey on the phone. He's trapped in the security building in there. He says he's sure seven of his officers got it. He's safe enough where he is and is sitting tight."

"Any chance of evacuating the animals?" McNeal asked, "maybe setting up the high pressure hoses to stop the spiders long enough to—"

"You're kidding. Nothing'll stop those bastards once they start moving. Even if we could, you ever try to handle a bunch of wild animals out of their minds with terror?"

McNeal looked through the main gate into the tree-shrouded interior of the zoo. Everything seemed quiet and peaceable enough. "Got any idea what's goin' on in there?"

"I sent some unwilling volunteers in there to check out what we're up against. The officer who came back with a report was as shaken as I've ever seen a man . . . the look on his face was enough to give you the willies. He refused to go back in there, even under direct orders. Can't say I blame him . . . those goddamn spiders covering everything, milling around in there . . . looking for food, I guess, or feeding on whatever they've found. What really worries me is what the hell they're going to do after they've—"

A uniformed sergeant came stumbling out the main gate. "They're movin' again, comin' this way!" he shouted, pointing behind him and then running off as fast as he could toward the parking lot.

Bryson jumped down from his perch on the cement rim of the fountain, as the first of the spiders came pouring out through the main gate of the zoo. Everyone ran. Men already in the parking lot jumped into vehicles and rolled up the windows. McNeal ran as fast as his weight would allow him. If he lived through this he'd never forget his first sight of those monstrous spiders pouring down the cement steps, barely ten feet behind him. . . . He saw Bryson pass him like the man was shot out of a gun.

The spiders quickly gained on McNeal. He felt sharp, stinging pains on his ankles, then his thights. He could feel their claws right through his clothing as they crawled up his back and onto the roundness of his belly. He knew if he tripped or fell down he was dead . . . they'd finish him in a matter of minutes. They were clawing at his neck, were in his hair. He glanced to his right, decided he had only one chance. . . . He jumped as hard as he could to the right, using all the strength he could get from his legs, and went a short distance through the air to land in a huge belly flop in the middle of the lily pond, sinking like a rock in about five feet of water. He held his breath and stayed under as long as he could. He could still feel the stinging and squirming on his body. Finally he could hold his breath no longer. He came to the surface, sputtering and gulping air in the midst of floating dead spiders. He waded to the edge of the pond, his clothes dripping wet, his hair hanging in his eyes.

A few firemen were manning the high pressure hoses, trying to help the men that couldn't outrun the advancing spiders.

"Hey," McNeal yelled, waving his arms frantically. A moment later a powerful gush of water cleared the way for him and he somehow managed to climb over the rim of the fountain, then stumble toward the parking lot. He got to Bryson and three other officers sitting inside a police car. Dripping wet, he scrambled onto the front seat next to Bryson.

The night was alive with screams and shouting as men were overrun and trapped in a sea of clawing, biting death. Some police officers in their panic drew their weapons and fired into the mass of spiders, which, of course, did absolutely no good. When the spiders overran a man, within a matter of seconds he was nothing more than a twitching, jerking corpse. There was nothing any of them could do . . . just sit and watch it happen.

"Where's Sergeant Williams?" McNeal asked, looking around.

"Haven't seen him," Bryson said. "I thought he was with—" And then there was no need to talk as they spotted the tall figure of Williams running at a right angle away from the advancing rush of spiders, running hard, head down, feet pumping . . . until suddenly he stumbled over one of the water hoses, went down hard on his knees, then onto his face. He tried to get up, but it was too late—the advancing wave of spiders swept over him.

"Good god," McNeal was saying . . . "I—I can't just let him . . ." He drew his revolver, sighted at the screaming, kicking figure.

"George, you can't—" Bryson grabbed for the gun.

"I've *got* to," McNeal said, pushing the hand away. And then there was a loud report from McNeal's gun, and the squirming figure on the ground lay still.

McNeal slowly reholstered his gun. He turned to Bryson, waiting.

Bryson looked at him for a long moment, then at the other officers, all looking off in a different direction. "I didn't see a thing, nobody did."

"Thank you, Frank—" McNeal began, and was interrupted, as more shouting echoed in the distance and they heard an officer call out, "Those sons of bitches are heading toward the Golden State Freeway. . . ."

They quickly started their engines, and the area was filled with a metallic clanging as the spiders, caught up and decapitated by the fast-moving fan blades, bounced about under the hoods of the police cars as they drove quickly through the blanket of spiders toward the freeway, leaving a trail of squashed, squirming bodies. They had to get to the freeway before the spider army did.

They sped now along Freeway Drive, heading for the Zoo Drive on-ramp, a string of nine police cars, sirens screaming. Bryson and McNeal were in the lead car, Bryson radioing orders to the other units. The steady onrush of spiders was already approaching the grassy apron that skirted the freeway, a moving black carpet of crawling bodies as far as the eye could see off to the right of the speeding police cars. They were now scarcely a quarter of a mile away from the freeway.

The sun was just beginning to peak over the top of the Burbank hills. It was dawn. Bryson hung up the microphone, sat shaking his head. He looked at his watch. "Six o'clock on a Friday morning," he said, almost to himself. "The heavy traffic's going to start soon, heading for the city." He looked at McNeal. "If we don't somehow stop that traffic . . . there's going to be a goddamn catastrophe—"

"A roadblock," McNeal said. "It's our only hope."

"Have we time?" Bryson said, nonetheless reaching

for the mike. "Those SOB's are really coming fast." He got on the radio, was patched through to the highway patrol. He gave quick, precise details, telling them exactly what was needed. As he spoke, highway patrol units were already speeding to their location.

They came out at the road junction, then along the frontage road to the right, heading for the freeway on-ramp. McNeal could now see the spiders, advancing at a good pace toward them.

They sped up the Zoo Drive on-ramp at about sixty miles an hour. At least, McNeal thought, glancing down the freeway, there wasn't much traffic yet, just a few cars and trucks that maybe, just maybe they could stop with bullhorns and a lot of arm waving.

They came to a screeching halt on the shoulder of the freeway and piled out of the police cars, the men in each unit digging into the trunks and coming up with flares, bullhorns, anything they could find that might help to stop the traffic.

McNeal, arms loaded with flares and equipment, glanced off to his right—too late . . . the beginning wave of the flood of spiders was already moving down the embankment and onto the freeway.

A plumber's truck, coming south at some sixty-five miles per hour, was the first vehicle to pass. The driver, startled out of a monotonous drive by the line of police cars and blaring bullhorns, cut to the inside lane of the freeway, abruptly saw the mass of spiders fifty yards ahead. He slammed on his brakes and cut the wheel sharply to the left, hoping to avoid what was advancing in front of him. He hit the cement center divider with a rasping crunch of his left front fender and went scraping and sliding along the center fence, the impact and jolt sending pieces of pipe flying in all directions onto the freeway. He came to rest, to be immediately smacked in

91

the rear by a woman driving a Ford station wagon. The woman was thrown against her steering wheel, then back against the seat. She sat with her head bobbing from side to side, obviously in a dazed condition. After a moment she seemed to come to her senses and began pushing frantically at her driver's side door. Every few seconds she would turn and seem to be fussing with something on the seat next to her, then start pushing against the jammed door again.

The man in the plumber's truck was thrown from the truck as his door buckled and sprang open, and he lay sprawled on the concrete as police officers rushed onto the freeway to pull him to safety. He was unconscious and was put in the back seat of a police car.

McNeal could see that the woman had given up on the door and had picked up the blanketed bundle from the seat next to her. God . . . a baby. . . . He watched the advancing wave of spiders swarming under and around her car. She was trapped in her car with a baby. . . . He got on the bullhorn. "Stay in your car, roll the windows all the way up . . . you will be safe. . . ."

She did as he said, and after closing all the windows she sat with her baby cradled in her arms, tears pouring down her face and onto the front of her blouse.

The spider mass had now completely covered the southbound side of the freeway for about two hundred yards, swarming around the station wagon and truck piled up in the center. McNeal could see the woman looking around at them, the look of horror on her face. She was still holding the baby against her breast, rocking back and forth.

The spiders were scrambling over the cement bunker dividing the freeway, spreading out into the northbound lanes. The few cars coming in that direction swerved or changed lanes quickly, and avoided the spiders. Most of

so intense it blistered the paint on the police cars, singed the hair and the faces of the officers.

Fire units arriving on the scene could do nothing to extinguish the flames while the spiders moved across the area.

"Just let the damn thing burn," was the word from the fire chief. "I'm not sending my men out there."

The advancing spiders were momentarily stopped by the burning gasoline as it flowed across the freeway and into the drainage ditch in front of them. They milled around at the edge of the fire line for a while, then began advancing again, moving to the right and giving the fire a wide clearance.

The burning gasoline stopped at the drainage ditch and ran down the sloping embankment before it could reach the police cars. A good thing that it did, Bryson thought . . . there was nowhere else they could run, sure as hell—not from here.

The highway patrol had finally succeeded in road-blocking the freeway in both directions, and traffic began backing up immediately. People were getting out of their cars to see what was happening, some climbing up to sit on the roofs of their cars to get a better view.

There was nothing for the police and firemen to do but stand and wait as the fire burned itself out. Finally, after what seemed like hours, the last of the spiders cross the freeway and disappeared down the embankment on the other side.

The freeway was carnage . . . the station wagon and trucks, completely gutted, sat smoldering. There were great scorched spots on the highway, and everywhere McNeal looked he saw curled and crisp spiders covering the blackened concrete.

"What the hell do we do now?" Bryson muttered.

"Try to find out where those bastards are going,"

McNeal said, and started out across the freeway.

Frank caught up with him and they crossed the south-bound lanes of the freeway and went through the jagged hole in the chain-link fence. The smell was unbearable. McNeal had to press his handkerchief over his nose and mouth. Two uniformed officers caught up with them as they reached the top of the embankment, and they looked down across the dry riverbed of the Los Angeles river, where the last of the spider mass was crossing and disappearing into the large cement spillage openings to the storm-drain system—like a rush of black water flowing into a drain.

McNeal and Bryson exchanged a look, both thinking the same thing. Bryson put it into words. "Those god-damn tunnels stretch for hundreds of miles underneath the entire city," he said. "We'll never get them out of there."

"Don't worry," McNeal said dismally, "I'm sure we haven't seen the last of them."

They started back across the freeway toward their cars, being careful to keep out of the way of the firemen in-specting the smoldering damage and the two trucks removing the demolished vehicles. The freeway was still choked with cars and trucks for as far as the eye could see in either direction. It would all have to be cleared up and the freeway closed—the highway patrol's problem.

The television crews had set up their cameras just outside the area and had filmed everything that had hap-pened from four different directions. Newscasters were on the scene, still trying to get their interviews.

Nobody paid any damn attention to them. Bryson de-ployed officers all along the top of the embankment fac-ing the dry river basin and the drainage system openings to watch for the reappearance of the spiders but, more importantly, to keep the usual group of curious sightseers out of the area. Every tenth man was given a walkie-talkie, and at the first sign of spiders was to be in direct communication with a command post set up near the freeway; to do exactly what, nobody really knew. If the spiders did appear again, they were all still defenseless.

Bryson replaced the radio hand-mike and climbed out of his police car. He lit a cigarette, stretched. "I just finished talking with the high brass," he said disgustedly. "There'll be some high-level meeting later this afternoon. We're to attend. . . . Well, we've done all we can here. Let's go home and at least get a couple of hours sleep. When I find out the time for the meeting I'll call you." He got into his car, started the engine. "We've got a rotten afternoon ahead of us, George," he said, matching McNeal's dreary expression. "Not to mention a long night."

Chapter 12

IN THE city of Los Angeles, the people were awakened from a relatively secure sleep that morning by a mass assault of the news media proclaiming, with all the impact of an end-of-the-world announcement, that "Los Angeles has been attacked by an army of gigantic killer spiders!" The newspapers, forced to compete with on-the-spot radio and television news, were obliged to take what little actual information and facts they had and sensationalize it across their front pages with banner headlines: KILLER SPIDERS EXPECTED TO SLAUGHTER THOUSANDS! and IS LOS ANGELES DOOMED? Although no scientists were available for interview, one newspaper ran a front-page story entitled: SCIENTISTS AGREE—MAN-EATING SPIDERS COULD TURN LOS ANGELES INTO A GHOST TOWN! These headlines were all accompanied by the few actual photographs available, laid out in such a way as to fill the front pages. Unfortunately, the repeated photographs only served to give the pictorial impression of wholesale murder of hundreds of innocent people by the spiders.

The switchboards of every police station and fire department in the city were so bombarded with telephone calls they had to be temporarily closed down. Families by the thousands hastily packed their belongings and choked the freeways and roads in their panicky attempt to escape the city.

Radio and television news then moderated their tone after realizing the panic they had set in motion, stressing that the danger existed in a relatively small section of the city and that the greater part of Los Angeles had no cause to be alarmed . . . only a small portion of Glendale, a six-square-mile area extending from San Fernando Road to the Golden State Freeway would have to be evacuated and the freeway itself from Riverside Drive to Los Feliz Boulevard would be closed to traffic in both directions. People were advised not to attempt entering the evacuated area because a police cordon had been set up around its perimeter, sealing the area completely; no one would be allowed in.

The frequent "keep calm, don't worry" bulletins finally had their effect. People began returning to their homes, but they waited anxiously for the next on-the-spot telecast. The city was literally holding its collective breath over what would happen next, although by three o'clock that afternoon the situation had apparently been restored to a reasonably orderly state.

The mayor of Los Angeles called a special press conference to "personally inform the people as to the situation and the danger that exists . . ." He began by publicly reprimanding the news media for what he personally termed "a flagrant use of 'yellow journalism' at this time of the worst localized crisis." He also stated that the media had only generated panic and mass confusion.

"A very important meeting, scheduled for ten o'clock this morning," the mayor explained, "has already been delayed four hours due to the endless snarl of needless traffic. I have no choice but to blame the media for that."

"It is our job to inform the public," one reporter challenged.

Another spoke up: "Let's get down to facts, sir. Is this spider menace spreading throughout the tunnel system? In fact, is the city in imminent danger?"

"At this time," the mayor answered, choosing his words carefully, "I would say no. The spiders seem to be confined to a relatively small part of the tunnel system. I've been advised by people who are experts on the characteristic and behavior patterns of creatures such as these, and it's their opinion that the spiders entered the tunnels seeking a familiar refuge and will stay where they are, for the time being at least. I can assure you everything possible is being done to keep any potential danger to a minimum, to keep this thing as contained as possible."

"Are you referring to that police cordon, the one set up around that area?" a reporter asked. "What can they do to stop spiders?"

"Nothing," the mayor answered. "They're a peace-keeping force, to keep the curious and especially vandals and looters out of the evacuated area. The measures of containment I was referring to include placing drums of a jellied incendiary mixture—much like napalm—in the tunnels, completely encircling the perimeter. These drums can be exploded and ignited electronically by police officers who have gone down into the tunnels through manholes to act as spotters. They are a safe distance, not only from the drums but from the spider mass. At the first sign of activity or movement by the spiders, the drums will be detonated, filling that section of the tunnel with burning petroleum."

"Are you sure this burning napalm will destroy the spiders?"

"I'm not sure," the mayor answered honestly. "There's a meeting scheduled in about two hours to discuss it, and everything else about this awful business. At the moment this petroleum mixture would only be used as a deterrent—to stop them from advancing any further than the perimeter."

"Where did these spiders come from?" a reporter asked. "How in the world did all this get started?"

The mayor threw up his hands. "Truth to tell, gentlemen, I just don't know." And noting the skeptical looks, added, "I can assure you *nothing* in this matter is being hidden or covered up. As soon as I have some answers to your questions I guarantee you will all be informed." He looked at his watch. "Now, if you will excuse me . . ." He left the podium and exited through a rear door.

The reporters hurried to a bank of telephones at the rear of the small auditorium to phone in what little they had to their respective papers.

MCNEAL WAS washing up in the men's room just before the meeting was to start. He heard the door behind him open and close, then a nasal voice he vaguely remembered.

"Oh, Lieutenant . . . ah, McNeal, wasn't it? I was told you would be here today and I was hoping to find you alone . . . there's something I'd like to say to you. . . ."

McNeal felt the anger rise in him, along with full recollection. He had trusted Dr. Benjamin's integrity, had finally believed him. Maybe if he had gotten truthful answers at the time this horrible thing might have been prevented. He turned around slowly.

"You can't possibly do or say anything to me that I don't deserve," Benjamin was saying, and McNeal, looking at him, realized he meant it.

"You blame me for what's happened. I blame myself. Except . . ." He took a deep breath. "Lieutenant, I have a schedule that sometimes doesn't leave me time to breathe, you came to me with a bag of mangled specimens and a death report. At the time they were nothing more than a nuisance to me—you were a nuisance. I ignored it, and you . . ." He took another deep breath, wiped his face with a handkerchief. "This morning I got a telephone call from a Dr. Perelli of the health department. He asked my aid in this busines, told me where and how it had happened. I was shocked by what he told me. A little late, I grant you . . . and then I remembred—remembered your visit, the strange homicide you told me about. You suspected something bizarre even then, and asked my help. True, there was little or nothing I could have actually done with those damaged specimens, but I should at least have tried. Instead, I acted like a pompous ass, and except for a cursory examination, ignored it completely." He shook his head in disbelief. "Lieutenant, does all this that's happened really stem from—?"

"Yes, doctor, I'm afraid it does."

"Then God help me—I'll have to live with it." Dr. Benjamin took on the look of a man totally beaten by his own conscience.

"It's something we'll all have to live with, you, me,

everyone connected with this thing," McNeal told him. "There's blame enough to go around. I should have dug deeper in checking out that autopsy report and what the ME showed me instead of being so goddamn anxious to write it off as an accidental death. We *all* share the responsibility. Now, the real question is—can you do anything to help? . . ."

"Lieutenant, I'm pretty expert in my field. I'll do my damnedest."

"I'm sure you will," McNeal said, but please hurry." He looked at his watch. "I think we should get back to the conference room before they start without us."

In the conference room Mayor Bradshaw seated himself at the head of the table. "Gentlemen," he said in a deep baritone, "considering the gravity of the situation, this meeting should have been held this morning. I can imagine what you've all been going through. I had to be flown here from my car stuck in traffic on the Hollywood Freeway. I'm glad you all made it. I had hoped that Governor Harris could be here"—he looked slightly embarrassed—"but unfortunately the governor was busy with . . . other matters and couldn't be located until just an hour ago. He's promised to fly to Los Angeles as soon as possible." He turned and began a whispered conversation with Chief Richardson.

McNeal glanced at the other men seated around the conference table, most of whom he recognized. Mayor Bradshaw at at the head of the table, Chief Richardson sat on his right, Dr. Perelli on his left. Of course he knew Bryson and Dr. Benjamin, who were seated across from him. He recognized MacCandell from the city engineer's office, and Battalion Fire Chief Gilbert at the far end of the table. He didn't know the two men seated on each side of him. He introduced himself and learned the man on his left was H.L. Haskel, president of Globe-Eastern Extermination, Incorporated; the man on his right, T.W. Bates, head of M-J-T Extermination Company. By the way they talked it was soon obvious that they were old rivals.

Mayor Bradshaw ended his private conversation with Chief Richardson and turned to face the group.

"Gentlemen," he said without prologue, "thirty-five people were killed in that horror early this morning." He referred to a sheet of paper in front of him. "Eighteen police officers, eight firemen, nine civilians, including a young mother and her four-month-old baby. I'm afraid this is only the beginning if this thing gets loose in the city at large—"

"It *is* loose," McNeal interrupted. "We discovered what was happening too late, didn't realize what it really was, what it meant—"

The mayor held up his hand. "We're not here to put blame on anyone. We only—"

He was interrupted by a knock on the meeting room door.

A woman entered, carrying a thin attaché case and dressed in a tailored pantsuit, hair neatly framing her round face. McNeal judged her to be in her early fifties.

"Excuse me for barging in like this," she said breathlessly, as if she had been hurrying, "but I think I have some information that may be of some help. I am Dr. Selby. . . ."

Dr. Benjamin got slowly to his feet. "Dr. Christine Selby?"

"Yes."

"I know you by reputation, doctor." He turned to the mayor. "Dr. Selby is a world-renowned expert in entomology and arachnology."

"Under the circumstances," Mayor Bradshaw said,

"you're more than welcome, doctor. What information were you referring to?"

"It is what's been happening, or at least I suspect has been happening concerning the project that I'm working on. The project is classified top secret by the government, and I'd rather not give any specifics on the work until I'm reasonably certain that the information is pertinent to the present situation."

The mayor looked confused. "As you wish, doctor," he said. "We were just discussing the situation when you arrived."

The mayor separated a stack of manila folders in front of him. "Lieutenant McNeal has compiled a report on the evidence and events leading up to this morning's tragedy. I've mimeographed a copy for each of you." He passed the reports around the table.

They took a few minutes to quickly study McNeal's report. McNeal answered questions. On the whole, the report was detailed enough to give them a good idea of what had occurred regarding the sequence of deaths and missing persons reports.

The mayor got to his feet again. "Dr. Benjamin, can you tell us anything about the nature of the menace we're facing? . . . Dr. Benjamin is Professor of Arachnology at the University of California," he added by way of introduction.

Dr. Benjamin got slowly to his feet, adjusted his glasses. "If the information in the report I've just read is accurate, then, no, I'm afraid I really can't tell you very much about this species of arachnid you're referring to as 'the menace.' The behavior patterns of this species is contrary to anything known at this time. I can't even venture a guess as to origin or characteristics. They are like nothing I, or anyone else, has ever seen before."

"I've seen, and worked with, specimens similar to

these," Dr. Selby said in a low voice. "I'm part of the scientific team that produced them. I apologize for having been so mysterious before but I had to make absolutely sure of the facts before I could release any classified information. If what *I've* just read and heard is true, then I'm sure beyond any doubt that they are of the same mutant species."

"You—developed them?" Dr. Benjamin asked incredulously.

"Yes. Or at least a species strikingly similar to them . . . it's been a known fact for many years that the ozone layer surrounding the earth is slowly deteriorating and someday will disappear entirely. This ozone layer, among other things, filters out and prevents large bombardments of ultraviolet and gamma rays from striking the earth. Since it's a foregone conclusion that the ozone layer will eventually dissipate, and these bombardments will occur, it's the great concern of the scientific group I'm presently working with as to exactly what effect this concentration of ultraviolet and gamma rays will have on plant and animal life. I'm presently heading a government project set up in the Mojave desert to test and record these effects. We've set up a series of near-perfect environments, duplicating as nearly as possible every climatic and regional difference. In these environments are samplings of every major plant and animal species in the world. Each environment is separate and enclosed in its own sheet-steel enclosure, and for twelve hours each day they are continually bombarded with high-intensity ultraviolet and gamma rays." She paused and looked at Dr. Benjamin, as though she were talking directly to him. "For one of the environments, we simply left a four-acre piece of desert in its natural state, representing the American desert. It is complete with every plant and animal representative of the desert—including the desert tarantula."

"Then you believe that one or more of these specimens escaped into the desert?" Dr. Benjamin asked.

"No . . ." She paused and seemed to be reconsidering her answer. "At least I'd think it highly unlikely. These enclosures are designed so as to make the possibility of escape really out of the question. As I've said, the walls are constructed of heavy gauge sheet steel, riveted together at all joints and sections. The base of the walls is buried in eight to ten feet of earth, depending on the terrain. Also, each of the specimens is classified and numbered according to its particular species and group. Each group is examined and, if necessary, reclassified once a month. I personally examine the spiders and insects of the desert group."

"Then we can rule that out as a possibility?" Dr. Benjamin asked. "When these examinations take place, all the classification numbers are in sequence, and you've found none missing?"

"Well, no . . ." Dr. Selby answered, a little hesitantly. "There are variables to consider. Perhaps a specimen dies, or can't be coaxed out of its burrow, and is passed over until the next examination. But eventually all the specimens will be accounted for. . . ." She hesitated and looked thoughtful for a moment. "There was one incident, but it happened well over a year ago, and was so minor I suspect it's hardly worth mentioning—"

"What was that?" Dr. Benjamin pressed.

"During a violent desert storm the extremely high winds caused the riveted seam between two sections of the wall to buckle and separate. Whenever something like that happens, an alarm sounds. Within less than half an hour the maintenance crew had the wall sealed again and to my personal knowledge not a single specimen escaped." She gave a little shrug. "I still maintain that escape from our facilities would be nearly impossible."

"Nonetheless," Dr. Benjamin said, "you do suggest a similarity between these specimens and our spiders. What is it?"

"Only that in the last two years the tarantula specimens have shown a marked increase in their aggressiveness and tendency to colonize. No other differences have been discovered or brought to my attention. If possible, I'd like the opportunity to examine one of these creatures."

Dr. Perelli gestured to get Dr. Benjamin's attention. "Professor, inspectors from the health department and myself were out at the Griffith Park Zoo earlier this afternoon. We found quite a few of those creatures trapped in various places such as ditches, holes, and the bottom of trash cans. We managed to capture roughly three dozen specimens by using elbow-length leather gloves. I assure you, doctor, leather gloves are a necessity in handling them. I couldn't believe the ferocity of these damn things. In any case, your facilities at the university are certainly superior to ours at the health department, not to mention your knowledge in the field, so I've taken the liberty of sending the specimens directly to your laboratory. They should arrive shortly, if they are not already there."

"Excellent," Benjamin said and turned to Dr. Selby. "Doctor, I'd consider it an honor if you'd work with me on this."

She quickly agreed.

Dr. Perelli of the health department wanted to know ". . . if these creatures carry any type of disease or parasitic organism, and is their bite toxic?"

Benjamin said he had no way of knowing until he and Dr. Selby had made a round of internal and external tests. All he could say with any certainty was what was already known about the species and he proceeded to lay it out for them.

"Basically, all Arachnida—all spiders—are divided into two distinct groups. Araneomorphs, or true spiders, a highly evolved and advanced order; and Mygalomorphs, a primitive, more basic order. It's the latter that we're dealing with here. Mygalomorphs would be considered the barbarians of the spider world. Unlike their tiny aristocratic cousins they're huge, powerful, ground-hunting brutes. I have seen specimens of the South American variety with bodies measuring three inches in length and having a leg-span of another ten to twelve inches. This variety has been known to attack and kill small rodents, and even catch birds. Again, unlike their daintier relatives, mygalomorphs—or, in this case, tarantulas—do not rely on a webbing network in order to trap their prey but rather on speed and brute strength; their fangs and chelicerae can easily crush even the largest of insects. Their venom is not fatally toxic, it affects their victim's nervous sytem, having a paralyzing effect. To my knowledge, there has never been a single fatality in this country due to a tarantula's bite, although their fangs can produce a painful bite."

He picked up the report again. "A fact that completely mystifies me, especially in view of what happened this morning, is that these creatures have always been known to be quite timid when they come in contact with man. They've only been known to bite when cornered, or provoked. Why, in the South American countries, young children tame them and keep them as pets; they even respond to petting and affection. Believe me, gentlemen, if what Dr. Selby here says is true and these spiders have no relationship to the specimens she's been studying, then I have absolutely no way of explaining the almost bloodthirsty aggressiveness they've displayed."

"Are you suggesting that we are dealing with an entirely new species?" Dr. Perelli asked in amazement.

"No. A new species isn't born overnight. A complete evolutionary change takes many thousands of years," Dr. Benjamin explained. "What I do suspect is a highly specialized genetic change in their social and reproductive patterns."

The mayor said, "I was under the impression that this entire business was caused by a huge explosion in the spider population, but that the spiders themselves were, well—ordinary spiders."

"It's this population explosion itself—this massing of them—that makes them so unique, and dangerous." He glanced at Dr. Selby, who was nodding in agreement. "Let me state the facts as clearly as I can. Tarantulas live solitary lives. You will never find two of either sex living in the same burrow. They're extremely long-lived, and not at all migratory, sometimes living for twenty-five or thirty years in the same hole and never venturing more than ten feet in any direction from it. Their eyesight is quite poor and they're unable to see more than five or six inches in front of them. But poor eyesight is more than made up for by their acute hearing and sensing organs, made up of hair follicles covering their entire body that enable them to sense movements up to forty feet away. These spiders are, by their very nature, cannibalistic. They would just as readily kill and feed on one of their own kind as any insect or rodent. It's quite common for a mother to hatch a brood of six to nine hundred spiderlings, then devour most of them. Statistically, out of a brood of nine hundred babies, only three or four ever reach maturity. And maturity for these spiders usually takes seven to ten years. Do you understand what this means?" He looked around the table at the blank

111

faces. Only Dr. Selby seemed to appreciate the implications, by the astonished look spreading across her face.

"Let me explain in a little more detail. For the first four months of the new spiderling's life it can't even feed itself, so they are totally dependent on the mother. Then they go through the first of their molting stages, which means that their skin hardens and cracks, then peels away, and a little bit larger and more mature spider emerges. These spiders molt once a year after that, for their entire lifetime. Now, for close to the next two years, these spiderlings are in what I would describe as their infant stage. They can feed themselves but their senses aren't fully developed. They are not, at this point, able to move very fast, are not particularly strong; literally, they must depend on an insect almost crawling down into the burrow with them before they could catch it. Spiders live on a strictly liquid diet, and at this stage of their development these spiders would have a great deal of trouble piercing an insect's shell to suck out the body fluids." He paused. "That point, gentlemen, is of great importance."

"Why?" Dr. Perelli put in.

"Before attending this meeting I viewed a ninety-minute videotape of that abomination this morning taken by one of the news services. The spiders I saw in that film ranged in size from three to ten inches in diameter, but none of them—absolutely *none*—could be described as being in the infant stage! Don't you realize what that means? There were no infants!" He could see that Dr. Selby understood his point all too well by the look of shock on her face.

"No infants at all?" she asked in disbelief.

"That's right! I'm convinced that these spiders didn't even exist a year ago—they couldn't have! Yet every single one of those spiders was viciously attacking and

feeding on every living thing in sight—*except* each other.
Being cannibalistic, they should have thought nothing of
setting upon and slaughtering each other. Instead they
seemed to be conducting themselves as a cooperative
colony, in the same fashion as ants and bees. It's impossible, but there it is, and I can't explain it."

"These spiders did exist a year ago," McNeal said,
pointing to his report. "We had definite proof of that at
the time. We just didn't take the time to check it out
thoroughly enough . . . because it seemed so impossible."

"Yes, yes, lieutenant, I remember that," Benjamin
said, hoping to dismiss a subject painful to his memory.
"And I still maintain that these facts are impossible."

"That's exactly what you said at our last meeting when
I showed you the same evidence," McNeal said, reaching
into his briefcase and producing the series of photographs taken by the medical examiner's assistant during
the autopsy. They clearly showed the spider egg casings
embedded in the dissected kidneys. He handed the
photographs to Benjamin, then turned to the mayor.
"The medical examiner who performed the autopsy on
the Miller boy believes the spiders originated in the form
of eggs introduced through the bloodstream, which
hatched inside the boy's body," McNeal explained. He
turned back to Benjamin. "Perhaps, in the light of everything that's happened since, you might be able to come
up with a better explanation."

After scrutinizing the photographs and referring again
to the report, Benjamin shrugged. "I have no answer,
lieutenant," he stated simply. "I just don't know. What
might have seemed totally impossible a year ago, now—
I don't know." He handed the pictures to the mayor for
the others to look at, then got to his feet. "Until we
dissect and test those specimens at my laboratory I can't

be of any further help to you. There's just nothing more I can tell you," he said in a tired voice.

"I have just a few more questions, professor," Mayor Bradshaw said. "Did I understand correctly a moment ago? You knew of the existence of these murderous spiders a year ago, and did nothing about it?"

"Well, that's not quite true, your honor," Dr. Benjamin said. "The lieutenant here came to me with an autopsy report and asked my opinion. I gave it to him, based on my best knowledge and experience. The medical examiner had stated in his report that spider eggs had, somehow, been injected into that boy's bloodstream. Based on everything I knew to be true, this would not have been possible, and I told him so—in the same way as if he had asked if spiders could fly, I would have said, impossible."

"But the spider samples themselves should have told you something, shouldn't they?"

"Except for their great size, the chief differences we are dealing with here are internal differences," Benjamin said. "The samples the lieutenant brought me were mangled and crushed almost beyond recognition. I honestly don't think they could have told me anything about how they functioned internally, but of course I'll never be sure now. . . ."

Walking with him down the hall toward the elevator, Dr. Selby told him not to judge himself, or them, too harshly. He was, she felt, right, and their pressing him only reflected their distress and fear at what they were facing, at the life-and-death decisions they had to make.

"Do you think they really understand the implications?" he said to her. "What the repercussions could be if they're not totally annihilated immediately?" He turned and looked at her. "Do you?"

"Yes. I'm afraid I do," she answered seriously. "Each of the female mygalomorphs in that colony could, theoretically, multiply by nine hundred or a thousand—with no loss of offspring at all from cannibalism. The offspring would quickly grow and mature, and in turn reproduce, again and again and again. And at that point there would be no way on earth to stop them."

". . . and I also think Dr. Benjamin has overplayed the seriousness of this situation," T.W. Bates stated to the other men seated around the conference table. "A population explosion such as this in the animal or insect world is not an uncommon phenomenon. In varying degrees it happens just about every year throughout the world . . . the swarm of locusts invading a field in China, Japanese beetles, boll weevils, and cutworms attacking crops right here in this country. It's not widely known, but I think Mr. Haskel will bear me out"—Bates said, nodding toward H.L. Haskel, who was sitting on the other side of McNeal with a look of distaste on his face—"every year just before winter there's a huge population explosion of cockroaches in most of the larger cities that goes almost totally unnoticed because most home and apartment owners believe they're the only ones infested with them and they're ashamed to admit to their neighbors that they have cockroaches. I can assure you, though, especially at that time of the year, the extermination business is excellent. Now, admittedly, although these pests I've named are destructive to property they aren't to man, but the important point is—they *are* dealt with. . . ."

Bates paused for a moment, selected a news clipping from the pile in front of him. "Here's an item from a newspaper in England. About two years ago the poorer section of London was horribly infested with rats, definitely a threat to human life on account of spreading infection and rat bites. There were even reports of packs of these rats literally tearing small children to pieces. The local government did the only wise and sensible thing . . . they hired professional exterminators to go in and eliminate the problem. By the use of professional equipment and professional knowhow, exterminators eradicated the vermin within four days. And, gentlemen," Bates said with a sweeping gesture of his hands, "I guarantee that we can do the same here. With the correct use of pesticides and poison vapor, we can successfully kill every last one of those—"

"Not to mention the human population in that part of the city," Haskel interrupted heatedly. "Surely you realize that the pesticides and poison vapor would spread for miles through the drainage system, then rise up through sewer grates and manhole openings to pollute the atmosphere with toxic vapors even more deadly to people than those spiders. . . . What you're suggesting is idiotic—"

"Perhaps you're not familiar with the latest equipment," Bates said. "I was speaking of a high density chemical vapor, triggered automatically from pressurized canisters placed along the intersecting tunnel routes." He indicated various places on a blueprint of the aqueduct system spread out in front of him. "Mr. MacCandell of the city engineer's office agrees that these are strategic locations for the placement of the canisters to enable the toxic fog to reach all parts of the drainage system in that section. The chemical fog, being roughly three times heavier than air, would never rise more than two feet off the floor of the tunnel, which eliminates your objections, Mr. Haskel."

"I'm familiar with high density Cloredine canisters,"

Haskel said tightly, "but they're specially designed for use in closely confined or airtight areas. To release that fog in those open tunnels, with no way to control air currents could be disastrous." He turned to the mayor. "Surely you can't go along with this insane proposal?"

Mayor Bradshaw hesitated a moment. "Mr. Haskel, your objections to the use of the insecticide canisters aren't taken lightly. You are, of course, an expert in this particular field. But, let me remind you, so is Mr. Bates. Now, he assures us that the chances of the disaster you describe are almost nonexistent—"

"If even a single fatality results from your going along with this plan you'd all be guilty of murder," Haskel exploded.

"Mr. Haskel, Mr. Bates has suggested a course of action, and a good one at that, but if you have an alternative we're here to listen to it."

"A simple ammonia spray," Haskel said. "These spiders breathe through book lungs located on their undersides. A concentrated ammonia spray would have the same lethal effect on them as the strongest of pesticides. The same men that would have to go into those tunnels to place the canisters could be equipped with pesticide sprayers filled with a concentrated ammonia solution. This spray would kill these creatures just as quickly and completely as Cloredine, and even if the ammonia vapors did rise up into the atmosphere, they would be infinitely less harmful to the population—"

"That's ridiculous," Bates broke in. "An ammonia solution would have little or no effect on those spiders. If a simple solution like that really worked, then as exterminators we'd have no need for chemicals like Cloredine. I assure you, what Mr. Haskel is suggesting would be a waste of time when every minute is precious."

Mayor Bradshaw sat quietly, waiting.

"Mr. Bates is swayed, I'm afraid," Haskel said, "by the fact that Cloredine is an extremely expensive chemical to use in such a large area. It would represent an immense profit to his company—"

"That's ridiculous and insulting," Bates broke in. "I'm only considering the most practical, effective way of eliminating this menace. Aside from the fact that I genuinely believe an ammonia solution will *not* be effective, think of the volume needed in order to cover six to eight square miles of underground tunnels—maybe a dozen or more tank trucks, with all the equipment and pressure hoses that go with them. And how about manpower? We would be exposing perhaps thirty or forty men to real danger by sending them into those tunnels—and all unnecessarily. . . . Not only can I guarantee that the Cloredine will be one hundred percent effective against any of the creatures that come in contact with it, but only ten or twelve of the pressurized canisters will be needed to do the entire job and only two or three men will be needed to deliver them throughout that section of the tunnels. As you can see, Mr. Mayor, the Cloredine would not only prove to be more effective but also safer to use."

Mayor Bradshaw leaned back in his chair. After a few moments he finally came to a decision. "We'll go ahead with the Cloredine," he said flatly.

"But I've already explained the dangers—"

"That's just a chance we'll have to take, Mr. Haskel." He glanced around the table, hoping for some sign of agreement or reassurance. None was offered as the men sat silent around the table, staring at one another.

"We just don't seem to have any good alternatives open to us," the mayor said. "We can't take the chance of not being effective and allowing more innocent people to die—"

But Haskel had gathered up his briefcase and was

storming out of the conference room.

The mayor looked around the table again. "This is still an open meeting, and I would very much like to hear your opinions and suggestions." He spread his hands in a hopeless gesture. "Personally I just see no other options."

Chief Richardson agreed completely and promised that the police department would back him all the way with whatever he decided. MacCandell of the city engineer's office said he'd go along too. "I'm familiar with the tunnels and intersections running under that part of the city," he said, "and I don't see any other effective way of eradicating them."

"We could try flooding them out," Battalion Chief Gilbert suggested. "Between the high pressure fire equipment under my command, and releasing the spillage control valves at Hansen Dam, water would flood the dry riverbed, then the tunnels—"

"The drainage system is designed to empty water out into the riverbed," MacCandell broke in. "In order to flood those tunnels the way you're suggesting you'd first have to flood the entire riverbed—some twenty-seven miles of it—and almost to overflow level before the water would rise high enough to reach the deepest parts of the tunnels. That would be impossible."

McNeal and Bryson suggested waiting to see what Dr. Benjamin and Dr. Selby could come up with, but Dr. Perelli pointed out that analyzing and testing the specimens, then discovering a workable antidote based on the test results could take weeks or even months. "What we need here is an immediate plan of action. I'm inclined to agree with Mr. Bates' proposal, to try extermination."

"What about the liquefied petroleum we've put in the tunnels?" Bryson asked. "I would think a flood of burning gasoline would be effective. We could add more drums, completely saturate the tunnels with—"

"The use of those petroleum drums would have to be reserved as a last-ditch effort," MacCandell said. "I grant you the burning petroleum would probably be effective, but it would be awfully dangerous. As you can see on these blueprints, the tunnels are laced with interconnecting gas mains and pipes. Even if the exploding drums didn't rupture and ignite those gas pipes, the tremendous heat generated by the burning liquid would. The result would be a holocaust of burning natural gas spreading throughout the city."

"And," the mayor put in, "these damn things seem to be staying as a colony, at the moment at least, confining themselves to a relatively small section of the tunnel system. Exploding the drums and the flow of burning liquid would force them to scatter throughout the tunnel system. Whatever means of extermination we use must be done while they're still in a confined, concentrated mass." He turned to Bates. "How quickly can you begin?"

"Well . . . the specialized canisters will have to be flown in from our San Francisco facilities. At least four specially trained technicians will need briefing on the correct placement of the canisters. . . ." He glanced at his watch. "It's nearly sundown. I'd estimate tomorrow morning, at the earliest. In order to be certain the extermination is complete, there should be a series of five applications covering the entire drainage system. . . . There are only two companies in this area large enough to handle this job—mine and Globe-Eastern. A few moments ago Mr. Haskel made it very clear he wants nothing to do with this course of action, which leaves my company," he said, spreading his hands, keeping his face straight.

"Not exactly," Bryson said. He turned to MacCandell.

"Are you familiar with the type of Cloredine insecticide canisters we were discussing? Can you locate what we need?"

"The city demolition crews use that chemical before clearing condemned buildings," MacCandell said, immediately getting the drift of Bryson's questions.

"But my company has all the equipment needed to—" Bates began.

Bryson ignored him. "As for the placement of the canisters, I can have a least a dozen volunteers for that assignment—"

"Volunteers aren't needed . . . as I've explained, I've trained technicians capable of—" Bates persisted, and was ignored.

"The men who go into those tunnels to place the canisters will need some sort of protective clothing from head to foot," McNeal pointed out. "Without it, they wouldn't stand a chance."

"The fire department has a specially constructed flame suit that's used in areas of intense heat and smoke," Chief Gilbert said. "It's chemically treated heavy-duty canvas triple-lined with asbestos insulation. It's a one-piece unit, including leather and vinyl-molded boots and a hood fitted with a shatterproof Plexiglas face shield. The whole suit is sealed airtight by gaskets and shielded zippers, and is also fitted with an oxygen tank. The damn thing is heavy—weighs about a hundred and ten pounds—but you could probably walk on the moon with it."

"It sounds made to order for what's got to be done," Bryson said. "We'll need three of them in different sizes—"

"We only have two," Chief Gilbert said, "but the suits are expandable and can be made to fit any size."

Meanwhile MacCandell returned to the conference table after making a call. "We've got 'em," he announced enthusiastically, "we've got all the Cloredine canisters we'll need."

The mayor, obviously pleased, turned to Bates. "It seems you're not the only game in town after all, Mr. Bates. The city seems well equipped to handle this without you—and what I'm sure would be your exorbitant estimates."

"You must be out of your mind. You can't handle an operation like this yourself . . . handling these chemicals can be extremely dangerous, you need experts—"

"Mr. Bates, this has just become a closed meeting. Now, if you'll excuse us—the door is in that direction."

Realizing he'd glibly overplayed his hand, Bates finally gathered up his briefcase and left the conference room, slamming the door behind him.. . .

McNeal fidgeted in his chair. He still felt he should say something, make some alternate suggestion, but he was damned if he knew what. He didn't much like the mayor's plan, too many uncertainties, too last-ditch drastic.. . .

"Let me compliment all of you," the mayor was saying now, "for prompt action in organizing the situation. Not to mention helping the city to resist that man's callous profiteering. I truly believe we're doing the only thing possible in using the Cloredine—everything else we've discussed hasn't measured up.. . . Unfortunately, though, this will have to wait until morning.. . . Before the meeting I had a talk with Dr. Benjamin and he made it very clear that these creatures will become—active tonight. Since our only chance of success is to use the chemical when the spiders are closely confined and in a mass, we have no choice but to wait." He looked around the table. "Everything must be coordinated and ready by six o'clock tomorrow morning."

"Everything will be ready to go," MacCandell assured him.

122

"What do you mean by 'active'?" McNeal asked, still feeling apprehensive.

"Dr. Benjamin said the spiders come out at night to hunt food—"

"But what are we going to do to avoid another tragedy like we had this morning?"

"If they do come out tonight, there isn't very much we can do to control them," the mayor admitted. "As I understand it, other than activating the drums of jellied petroleum, the only thing even remotely effective against them is the fire department's high pressure hoses, and even that's limited. I would suggest a coordinated effort between the police and fire department to form a tight cordon around the general area. That part of the city has already been completely evacuated. Anyone caught trying to enter that area after dark will be subject to arrest. Keep everyone out—no exceptions."

"Chief Gilbert and I have already prepared for that," Bryson said. "If they do come out, it would have to be through the drainage system openings and into the riverbed. There would be no other way. We've already got that area covered with police cars and firetrucks, and we've set drums of the jellied petroleum in the riverbed itself. I also have a tight cordon of police officers stationed across the entire top of the embankment. Between burning them with fire and flooding them with water, there's not much chance they'll do any damage—"

"And if they travel the other way, spread out into the tunnel system under the city?" McNeal broke in.

"Then as a last resort we'll activate the petroleum drums in the tunnels," the mayor told him.

"And if that doesn't stop them?" McNeal persisted.

"Lieutenant," Mayor Bradshaw said, "in that event I suggest we pray .. . ."

123

Chapter 13

DR. BENJAMIN escorted Dr. Selby into the science building, and led her quickly past the public elevators to the one marked FACULTY USE ONLY. He pushed the button for the sixth floor.

Driving from City Hall to the UCLA campus he had made the mistake of taking Wilshire Boulevard through the department store district at rush hour and they'd spent an hour and twenty minutes stuck in the long snarl of bumper-to-bumper traffic. It was made worse by their eagerness to get to the laboratory and begin work analyzing and testing those fantastic specimens.

There were no laboratory classes scheduled on Friday evenings, so they would have the main lab all to themselves. Dr. Benjamin had his own private laboratory adjoining his office, but that lab didn't have nearly the facilities of the main one, where they could work undisturbed all weekend if necessary.

As they rode up in the elevator he asked her if she'd had lunch, she said no, and added that she wished he'd quit calling her Dr. Selby . . . they'd be working together and her name was Christine. He managed to get out that his was Harold and they shook on it.

"Now, what are the chances of us getting something to eat?" she said. She had a lovely smile.

"When we get to the lab, I'll telephone the campus cafeteria and have some food sent up," he promised. There was something about her that made him feel like a damned nervous schoolboy. Foolish, but there it was.

They exited the elevator on the sixth floor, turned right down the long hall, continued to the end, then turned left into the east-wing foyer.

"I hope those health department people took some care not to damage or kill any of the specimens," Dr. Benjamin said. "Live specimens would be of infinitely more value to us." He could see by Dr. Selby's expression that she was impressed with the showcased collection of insects and spiders that filled the foyer. "I collected and mounted most of these myself," he said rather proudly.

"It's a remarkable collection," she said.

The entire east wing was deserted, the classrooms locked up tight. Good, he thought. That was exactly the way he wanted it. They were assured of privacy and quiet and would not be disturbed by the usual procession of students or teachers asking his advice every two minutes.

They would have the science lab all to themselves—

He froze in his tracks, rooted to the spot. The large double doors to the main laboratory were standing open, and he could hear someone moving around inside.

"What is it?" Dr. Selby whispered.

"Shh. Someone's in the lab." He pointed to the double doors. "You stay here, I'll go have a look. If anyone is foolish enough to release those specimens—"

He moved cautiously forward . . . to discover the cleaning cart in the center aisle and the slouching old custodian in faded coveralls standing near the cart. He'd just brought something down from his lips and was tucking it away under a pile of cleaning rags. Thank god, he thought, it was only Johnnie. . . . Nonetheless, he was annoyed.

Signaling for Dr. Selby to follow, he moved quickly into the lab, telling Johnnie to leave, that he had important work to do, and startling Johnnie so that he dropped a bottle of ammonia he was holding.

"Don't do that, professor," Johnnie said, recovering from the shock. "A scare like that's enough to kill an old man like me." He leaned against a lab table to steady himself, his shaking hand against his chest. "I was just hoping to get finished in here so I could go on home early. Not feeling so good tonight."

"Then go on home if you like," Dr. Benjamin said. When Dr. Selby entered, he led her to a wall locker in the back of the lab.

"I'll just clean up this mess," Johnnie said, taking a mop from the cleaning cart. "I didn't mean to—"

"Did you touch anything?" Dr. Benjamin asked, his eyes sweeping over the lab and coming to rest on three long canvas bags lying on one of the back tables. The bags moved and bumped slightly.

"No, sir, professor. You know I never touch any of the stuff in here," the old man said, mopping up the spilled ammonia.

"I don't think he's touched anything," Dr. Selby said, removing her coat and handing it to Benjamin. "Everything seems to be in order."

"All right. Now please leave us alone," Benjamin said again, taking the coat and hanging it next to his in the wall locker, then handing her a white lab coat.

"What's in them bags, professor?" Johnnie asked, wheeling his cleaning cart out through the double glass doors. "They sure seem frisky."

"That's no concern of yours," Dr. Benjamin said with finality.

They went over to the table to look at the canvas bags. Each was double-tied with thick cord and had PROPERTY OF THE DEPARTMENT OF HEALTH stenciled on its side in black letters.

"All right, then. I'll just come on back later and finish my cleaning," Johnnie said, more to himself than anyone else, and the glass doors closed behind him.

Before disturbing the canvas bags containing the specimens they first prepared two vivariums by spreading a thin layer of sandy soil across their bottom, then fitting each one with a heavy wire-mesh screen across the top. The mesh screens were mounted on hinges and could be locked. Dr. Benjamin next prepared a glass-sided wooden box with flexible hoses attached to anesthetizing gas canisters. "My students refer to this as 'Benjamin's gas chamber,'" he told her. "When the glass lid is closed the box is completely airtight. I prefer examining and dissecting living specimens, and the anesthetizing gas makes them easier to work with."

Dr. Selby mixed a saline solution in a large beaker and set it on a lighted Bunsen burner to heat while Dr. Benja-

128

min laid out on a white surgical towel the instruments they would use in their dissections: scalpels, probes of various sizes, a set of tiny clamps and spreaders.

He took a moment to call the college cafeteria to try to get them some food. "They told me they were officially closed," he said, replacing the phone, "but I got them to send over some chicken sandwiches and coffee."

Dr. Selby was grateful.

He located a pair of thick leather gloves in the laboratory storeroom, awkwardly pulled them on well above his forearms; they felt clumsy and uncomfortable but from what they'd been told about these specimens the gloves seemed essential.

"Let me do this," he suggested. "We really don't know what kind of creatures we're facing inside those bags, and, well, I'd feel better being the first one to handle them . . . in case."

Reluctantly, she agreed.

He approached the canvas bags almost gingerly, the movement within them increasing considerably.

"They know we're here!" Dr. Selby said incredulously, hearing their clamoring activity as their claws scraped the rough canvas, or they brushed against it. "Imagine how well developed their sensing organs must be for them to be able literally to smell or hear us approaching, even though they're imprisoned in thick canvas. It's amazing!"

He carefully lifted one of the bags and carried it over to the table on which they had set up the vivariums. The turmoil inside the bag was unbelievable. And they were heavy, he thought to himself. Heavier than he had expected. Whether it was because of their activity, or just plain body weight, he wasn't sure—but they certainly felt heavy! How much could a dozen spiders weight?

He cautiously untied the cord from around the end of

the canvas bag and stuck the now open end into the vivarium. He took the bottom of the sack in both gloved hands and raised it up, shaking it vigorously as he did so.

Nine of the most gigantic tarantulas they had ever seen tumbled into the fifty gallon vivarium. They immediately began to explore the floor of the tank, to test the glass sides. The coarse hair across their backs bristled, and every time two would bump into each other they would rear back and spread their fangs challengingly. They were clearly agitated.

Dr. Benjamin removed the bag and looked inside. Four more large spiders clung to its bottom. He pushed the bottom of the bag out through the top, reversing it, and the last four joined the others on the floor of the tank.

"They're incredible," Dr. Selby said, in complete fascination. She leaned forward to have a better look at them through the glass. "These two over here," she said, pointing to two of the largest ones, "must measure at least twelve or thirteen inches across, leg to leg. Their configuration is perfect in proportion to their huge size. So beautifully well developed, symmetrically perfect—"

There was a blur of motion as two of the spiders struck at her but bounced hard off the unyielding glass onto their backs. They righted themselves immediately, and struck again.

Involuntarily, she jumped backward into Benjamin's arms. She stood for a moment clinging to him, steadying herself, then looked at the spiders. They stood by the glass, fangs still spread, and seemed to be looking right back at her, watching her—it was damned unnerving.

"Are you all right?" he asked, feeling her shiver slightly.

"I'll be fine," she said, moving self-consciously away from him. "Excuse me for jumping at you like that. They moved so quickly . . . it startled me." She regained her composure and got back to business. "These specimens bear no resemblance whatsoever to the mutants we've bred at the project. These are like none I've ever seen before." She eyed the other two canvas bags. "I feel fine now, I suggest we get back to work."

Dr. Benjamin released the rest of the spiders into the other vivarium, rechecking twice to make sure that none remained clinging to the inside of the bags. They then began an examination of the specimens, writing their notes and opinions in a notebook.

There were a total of thirty-nine specimens, ranging in overall size from six to thirteen inches, from what they could estimate by simply looking at them. Their estimated weight ranged somewhere between an ounce or two for the smaller ones, up to and probably exceeding four ounces for the larger specimens. They were not the characteristically skinny, stick-legged spiders—these were husky, almost fat, specimens, the larger ones having plump, rounded bodies almost the size of a small child's fist.

Their most outstanding feature, to Dr. Benjamin's trained eye, was the development of the head, which was very large, even for those tremendous bodies. The eyes were unusually large, and were placed close together near the front of the head. The chelicerae were long and powerful looking, each ending in a long, curved fang. Some of the fangs he estimated to be close to half an inch in length. After seeing these monsters firsthand, it was easy for him to understand the horror and panic they'd caused. God, to have millions of these creatures loose in the city. . . .

They completed their preliminary notes on the spiders' physical description, then, putting the notebook aside, they selected one of the specimens for dissection.

Dr. Benjamin carefully caught a specimen of average size with the use of a long-handled strong nylon net. The other spiders in the tank became frenzied with activity but soon calmed down as he quickly carried the struggling tarantula over to the anesthetizing chamber, where he gently forced it into the glass-enclosed box, then closed and fastened the lid.

He allowed the tarantula a few moments to explore and test the interior of the box, knowing it would eventually stop all movement, and stand perfectly still to sense its new environment. When it did, he gave the metering valve on the canister a quick half turn. There was a sharp hiss of gas, and the tarantula immediately collapsed onto its belly, and lay unmoving. He opened the top of the box and took the limp tarantula out, laying it belly-up on the surgical table next to his instruments. Dr. Selby taped the spider's legs down in a spread position while he set up a large, powerful magnifying glass and adjusted its tripod legs to give him a clear image. He adjusted his eyeglasses to be sure they wouldn't slip off his nose as he bent over, selected a short-bladed scalpel, and with one quick and practiced movement separated the tarantula's sternum and abdomen. . . .

THE POLICE radio crackled with static, then Bryson's voice came over on TAC-2. "Roving C.P. to One-L-Six-teen—over."

McNeal stretched and rubbed his eyes. It was useless trying to grab any sleep with that damned radio sounding off every five minutes. He hadn't had much sleep the night before, today had turned out to be a long drawn-out series of meetings and tactical conferences, and now, by 10:30 at night, he was dog-tired. He picked up the hand mike. "One-L-Sixteen to C.P.—go."

"George, I'm still getting reports of noise and possible

movement from the unit at the corner of Broadway and Glendale—over."

"All quiet in my sector—over," McNeal reported.

"All the reports I'm getting from along Glendale Avenue indicate they're on the move," Bryson said. "Same along Colorado Boulevard. But the spotters in the tunnels report seeing no visible movement."

"When and if the spotters do report seeing 'em coming, are we authorized to use the petroleum drums?" McNeal asked.

"Not without a personal okay from the mayor. I think we ought to widen the perimeter in sections one and three. Try to keep ahead of them, just in case—"

"I think we ought to leave the perimeter right where it's at," McNeal said, looking at his map. "See what happens—"

"If those things ever got past us . . . into the populated section. . . ."

"Frank, we've already widened the perimeter twice since this morning. If we widen it again we won't have enough men and equipment to seal it. They're going to do something damn soon, they've got to. When they do we'll know where they are. We can't evacuate the whole damn city waiting for them—"

"Switch to car frequency, see what's on the air," Bryson told him.

McNeal switched frequency and contacted the other units in his sector, switched again to TAC-2 and contacted Bryson. "I'm getting the same kind of reports now from my units. A lot of noise and sounds of movement from under the streets. Spotters still report seeing nothing. If anything happens I'll let you know."

An officer came up to the car holding a cardboard container. "Coffee and danish, lieutenant?"

McNeal took one of the steaming-hot coffees and all

133

three of the danish in spite of the reproachful look from the officer. Well, he was hungry. After finishing the last danish and brushing a lap full of glazed sugar crumbs onto the floor, McNeal radioed his other units again. The reports were the same. Scraping, clacking noises coming from the concrete tunnels under the streets but still no visible movement. The noises were amplified by the hollowness of the tunnels. Whether the great mass of spiders was actually on the move, or just milling around, nobody knew.

McNeal hoisted himself out of the car, stretched the cramps out of his legs and back. He zipped the field jacket up all the way, turned his collar up around the back of his neck. The late evening cold was beginning to settle in. It was going to be another long night. He leaned against the car and reviewed the situation. They had the riverbed and the tunnel entrances covered in force—the places most likely for the spiders to emerge when they surfaced in search of food. The spider mass was still confined within the evacuated area, and there was no way they could move or spread out of that area without being detected by the spotters in the tunnels around the perimeter.

Nothing to do but wait.

THEY SAT by the desk in Dr. Benjamin's office. Dr. Benjamin looked over their notes again—for the third time. He couldn't believe the physical characteristics they had discovered.

Their external examination of the tarantulas had shown a highly developed network of sensing and hearing organs covering their entire body . . . these spiders could sense even the slightest movement or vibration, at considerable distances. The pedipalp on each side of the head was equipped, strangely enough, with double gripping claws, used to catch and hold prey. Each of the other eight legs was equipped with single claws, sharp as little fishing hooks. The epipharynx comprising the three-sectioned mouth parts was lined with tiny sharp teeth designed to grip and serrate the flesh. The fangs were sharp and powerful, each with a connected venom duct—he'd have to be sure to have the venom analyzed later. Physically, there could be no doubt that these creatures were hunters and killers—god knows they were designed for it.

Internally, they were a marvel to behold: They had extremely well developed retina and optical nerves in the eyes, although the pupil was such as to make them strictly nocturnal. The "sucking stomach," usually only a weak organ used for extracting fluids from prey, was so encased in strong muscles it was transformed into a powerful sucking pump.

The most astounding thing of all was the amazing physical changes in the females' sexual and reproductive organs. Of the six tarantulas they had dissected and examined, five had been females. Of those five, three of them, the smaller and younger ones, had been hermaphroditic—they'd possessed both male and female reproductive organs and could bear fertile eggs. These hermaphrodites also possessed a hard, stingerlike protrusion on the underside of their abdomen—like a hard penis connected to the vaginal opening. No one had ever seen anything remotely similar.

Dr. Benjamin sat back and rubbed the bridge of his nose. "We were right, Christine," he said. "They're definitely an entirely new genetic species." He glanced down at the notes. "I'd estimate that within two, three generations the males will be extinct, and the *entire* population will be hermaphrodites. Mating and nesting seasons will no longer have relevance; they'd simply lay eggs whenever their cycle dictated. The offspring, in turn, would inherit these genetic traits from the parent." He spread his hands with a shrug. "The male-female relationship will be completely obsolete in this species."

"Judging by the size of the population and how quickly they seem to multiply," she said, nodding in agreement, "I estimate their egg cycle to be about every three months. That, together with their lacking an instinct for cannibalism, will soon have them multiplying at the astounding ratio of"—she scribbled some hasty figures on a piece of paper—"one to the millionth power." She looked at him seriously. "They have *got* to be stopped."

He gathered up his notes and they left his office to return to the main lab. As soon as they entered the lab the specimens got active, milling around in the vivarium and trying to attack them through the glass. Dr. Benjamin tapped his pencil on the glass side of the tank, then watched as the spiders went berserk with activity.

"They're so murderously aggressive," Dr. Selby said, shaking her head. "Aside from their obvious physical attributes, they respond to any circumstance or opportunity with such bloodthirsty aggression. It seems to be a basic part of their nature. A newly acquired instinct."

At her suggestion, Dr. Benjamin assembled a large Plexiglas enclosure and inserted a partition through its center. Dr. Selby carefully selected three of the smaller, younger female specimens—the hermaphrodites. She placed these in the enclosure on one side of the partition. He then went into a smaller room next to the main lab, where the experimental animals were kept. He selected a large male guinea pig, one with a reputation for being aggressive and bullying his brothers and sisters, and placed him on the other side of the partition.

The guinea pig took a brief moment to sniff his new surroundings, then scurried to one corner of the enclosure, where he huddled in fear, obviously sensing the imminent danger as he pushed himself tightly into the corner, baring his beaverlike teeth.

Dr. Benjamin handed Dr. Selby a stopwatch. "Set it for a maximum of ten minutes. I doubt if it will take any longer than that for them to take care of him."

She pressed the button on the stopwatch at the same instant that he raised the center partition. The spiders shot forward, each coming at their victim from a different angle. The guinea pig had time only to give one squeak of terror before it had fangs and claws embedded in its back and stomach and behind its neck. It gave a few feeble kicks and jerks, then its body stiffened and it lay still. The spiders then proceeded to feed.

Dr. Selby pressed the button on the stopwatch again. "Killed him in eight seconds!" she announced in disbelief. She looked at Dr. Benjamin as an idea came to mind. "Or have they? Could it be possible—"

He caught her meaning right away. Using the end of the nylon net as a prod, Dr. Benjamin quickly forced the spiders away from the body of the guinea pig, then trapped them behind the partition again. He picked up the body of the guinea pig, carried it over to the examination table, examined it with a stethoscope. The body was stiff and completely immobile, but he definitely detected a slight heartbeat and shallow respiration. "This animal is still *alive*—"

"Check its reactions for impairment or damage."

He checked the pig closely under the magnifying glass. The pupils of its eyes were extremely dilated but the eyes reacted to light and shadow. He tested its hearing; it reacted, if only slightly. He then gave the animal a complete physical examination. All bodily functions seemed perfectly normal, except for the total paralysis. "The tarantula venom must be extremely toxic," he told her,

137

"to so completely affect the nervous system and motor areas of the brain."

He returned the guinea pig to its cage, noting the exact time on a small chart in order to determine how long the paralysis would last. He then selected another guinea pig. They allowed the spiders to attack again, and this time feed on the second guinea pig. It took a total of twenty-seven minutes.

After removing the shriveled corpse of the second guinea pig, he gave it a cursory physical examination. As he'd suspected, the small body was completely empty of body fluids. He selcted a third test animal and placed it in the enclosure. When they raised the partition this time the tarantulas didn't rush forward to attack the frightened guinea pig but rather circled it slowly and deliberately. Finally, one of the spiders shot forward and sank its fangs into the animal, which became rigid almost at once. The spider carefully maneuvered the animal onto its side, and slowly and very deliberately stung it with the now stiffened protrusion on its abdomen. The spider then seemed to experience a series of jerking spasms. The other spiders were keeping their distance, leaving the one spider alone with her victim.

The two scientists watched in fascinated disbelief.

Dr. Selby was the first to speak. "It seems like a ritual of some sort. . . ."

"It certainly isn't a feeding process," Dr. Benjamin added. "That guinea pig is still very much alive."

Finally the spider crawled away and joined the rest on the other side of the enclosure.

"We have got to find out exactly what this specimen just did," Dr. Selby suggested. "And why they weren't interested in feeding on this guinea pig."

Dr. Benjamin caught the three spiders in his net and returned them to the tank with the others while Dr. Selby moved the inert guinea pig over to the dissection table, where she drew a blood sample, smeared a slide and examined the blood under a microscope.

"This is unbelievable," she said. "The blood is literally choked with tiny spider eggs."

They then began a methodical dissection of the guinea pig to see the full extent of invasion by the spider eggs.

As Dr. Benjamin removed each organ, Dr. Selby placed it in a separate glass container and labeled it. They discovered spider eggs, or at least traces of them, in the heart, kidneys and the large and small intestines; they were present throughout the entire circulatory system. Were these spider eggs to hatch in the animal's system? If so, how long would it take? Did the host need to be living? Could these eggs incubate and hatch within a dead body? He thought of the human victims of these spiders . . . could those bodies contain incubating spider eggs, waiting to hatch—?

"Incredible," Dr. Selby said, looking up from the microscope. "These creatures impregnate their victim with fertilized eggs . . . the same way the Pepsis wasp uses them as host for its eggs. I've seen a tarantula hawk, a wasp a quarter the size of the spider it was fighting, fight and kill a large tarantula for the sole purpose of implanting a single egg in its body . . . the body of the spider would then be used as food for the emerging larva. . . ."

"Look at that," Dr. Benjamin said, pointing to the vivarium, where some of the spiders had flattened themselves against the glass side and were poking at it with their stingers. "They're trying to penetrate the glass."

He took a bookend from the shelf behind him and, going to the vivarium, placed it inside the tank. The bookend was made of soft wood and would serve the purpose, if he was right.

The same spiders that had been pressing against the glass immediately converged on the wooden bookend, crawling over it and pressing their stingers into it. After a few moments, the spiders crawled away, now ignoring the bookend completely.

Dr. Benjamin quickly reached in and retrieved the bookend. Looking at it closely, he could see numerous indented punctures along its flat sides. He took a bladed probe and scraped one of the punctures, then examined the scrapings under the microscope.

"Spider eggs!" he said, giving Dr. Selby a look. "As I suspected, they use those stingerlike protrusions to deposit their eggs. They probably prefer a living host, but during their egg-laying cycle, if their drive is strong enough, they'll deposit their eggs in whatever . . . whomever . . . is available."

"Which is probably what they're doing in the tunnel system at this very moment, now that they've made it their home," she said.

Dr. Benjamin removed his glasses and rubbed his eyes. He looked at his watch. "It's well past two A.M.," he said in surprise. "We've been working for almost twelve hours straight. We're both pretty beat and I, for one, am starving. I suggest we take a break, eat something and get some rest. After a few hours sleep and a hot meal I'm sure we'll be much more alert and effective. We need to be."

She stifled a yawn, nodded in agreement.

"I'll have to call Dr. Perelli, and tell him what we've found out so far," he told her. "And suggest that the bodies of all the victims of these spiders be cremated."

He went to his office and, after locking in his briefcase all the notes they had taken, went to the phone and dialed Perelli's number. When he returned to the main lab a few minutes later, Dr. Selby had just finished putting the last of their equipment away.

"Old habit," she said a little self-consciously. "I hate to leave a messy lab even for just a few hours."

"I talked to Dr. Perelli," he told her, his voice filled with annoyance. "He's got two entomologists from the Smithsonian with him and they all want to meet with us right away." He looked apologetic. "I'm sorry, I guess food will have to wait."

"But this isn't the time to be delayed in our work. This means we won't be back until morning."

"They came especially to help out. I'm afraid there's no way we can refuse. . . . Tomorrow we'll begin work on an effective way to combat these creatures—if it's possible." He shrugged. "What could effectively be used against them? Insecticides and poison chemicals would be out because there are so many of them, and their location underneath the city. A parasitic organism harmful to those spiders would be ruled out for the same reasons." He shrugged again. "Then what? I can't think of a single—"

"A bacteriological culture?" she said excitedly. "Why, I can think of at least nine different cultures that *might* be effective . . . if even one of them proved to be lethal—"

"You're *right,*" and impulsively kissed her on the cheek. "That's what we'll work on."

He unlocked the refrigerated storeroom where the dangerous drugs and bacteriological cultures were kept and selected fourteen possible cultures. He set them in a stainless steel rack on the lab table next to their instruments. The refrigeration in the storeroom made the bacteria cultures inert, and they would have to sit out at room temperature for the night. The next morning they would be ready to use.

They glanced once more around the lab as they took off the stained lab coats and put on their jackets. Every-

141

thing seemed to be in order, the vivariums were closed and locked, the Bunsen burner turned off. He switched off the overhead lights as they went out the glass doors, locking the doors behind them.

"Are you staying at a hotel?" he asked, as they started walking.

"No, I didn't have time to make arrangements. I rushed to make that meeting as quickly as I could."

"Well, I live alone and my apartment isn't much, but, well . . . after the meeting you're more than welcome to . . . ah, share pot luck with me and stretch out for a few hours sleep," he finally managed to get out.

She stopped, then looked seriously at him. "Yes, thank you. I think I would like that very much," she finally said.

"I'm afraid my place will seem quite a mess," he hurried on. . . . "Ever since Ethel . . . she was my wife . . . ever since she died it just didn't seem very important—"

"Harold," she said firmly, "will you stop apologizing and making excuses for living alone. It's not necessary. I've lived alone half my life, I know what it's like. It's lonely."

"If it's not too personal," he said, finally relaxing a little, "how is it that you've never married?"

"A combination of being too involved in my work and, I suspect, just never meeting the right person." She smiled at him.

He nodded. "I can certainly understand that. . . . It's been very much the same for me. . . ."

She linked her arm in his and they continued on walking down the hall.

"Man, i'm hurtin' real bad. I gotta score soon or I'm gonna *die*," Jerry hissed through gritted teeth, rocking back and forth on the front seat of the Chevrolet. He wiped his sweaty face with a grimy handkerchief.

"Shut up, man, just shut *up* and be cool," Mike ordered, trying to quiet him down. "We just gotta wait a little longer, till that old son of a bitch is ready to close, then we hit him. We gotta wait till he's ready to count the money. . . ."

They had been sitting in the Chevrolet for over an hour, parked across the street from the liquor store, watching the old man moving around behind the counter.

Mike had cased this liquor store before. He knew that old man Kellerman cashed payroll checks on Friday and always had plenty of cash on hand. Tonight, just before closing, would be the best time for them to hit him. Being afraid to pull this holdup alone, he had picked up on this Jerry character in a bar. Now he was sorry he had; the guy was really wasted.

"Oh, man . . . I feel sick," Jerry moaned, holding both arms across his stomach and continuing to rock on the seat.

"You better get your shit together and fast," Mike snapped at him, as much out of fear as anger. "I need a guy I can count on, not some damn junkie outa the gutter."

"Hey, man, I'm sorry," Jerry whined. He tried to sit up straight on the seat and failed. "I won't give you no more hassle. I just gotta get my head straight, I'll be o-kay. . . ."

Get his head straight! Mike thought. This turkey's whole life was getting enough bread to buy his next fix. It was different with Mike. If he could pull this off he'd have enough money to blow this city, get away from that SOB Rizzio and those bloodsucking loansharks, go somewhere else, start over. . . . Rizzio had told him if he didn't have the money he owed by tomorrow he'd be

143

cold meat. He knew they'd do it, too. Well, just let him pull this off and he'd have money enough to take off for where they'd never find him. . . . He pulled the Saturday night special out of his jacket pocket. It was a cheap .38 revolver, one he'd picked up from a guy who knew a guy and probably so cockeyed he couldn't hit the side of a building with it. He checked the load and clicked off the flimsy safety, then jammed it into the waistband of his jeans.

He glanced again across the street. Old Man Kellerman was dragging his newspaper racks inside through the front door of the liquor store. He looked at his watch; quarter to two, closing time. He glanced up and down Colorado Boulevard and saw no cars coming in either direction. The streets had been completely deserted for the last couple of hours.

"Come on, turkey, shape up! This is it," Mike said sharply. He started the Chevrolet and swung a U-turn in the middle of the street. They piled out, leaving the car idling in front of the liquor store. They entered the store just as the overhead neon sign went off.

"I'm sorry, boys, I'm just closing up," the old man said, returning from the back of the store and going behind the counter.

"Ah, come on, pop. We just wanta grab a six-pack. Only take a minute," Mike said, forcing a grin on his face. He motioned to Jerry to stay by the front door.

"Why don't you boys go home, get a good night's sleep? You can drink beer tomorrow." He eyed the two of them suspiciously. "I think maybe you boys really better go home."

"Then how 'bout your bread, pop? How 'bout givin' us all your bread?" Mike said nervously, pulling out the gun and sticking it in the old man's face.

The old man recovered quickly from the shock of hav-

ing a gun pointed at his nose. He smiled at Mike benevo-
lently. "My friend, listen to me a minute," he said softly,
a look of fatherly concern on his face. "Don't be a
schmuck. Don't do it. What'll you get? A few lousy dollars? You'll get caught and you'll go to jail, is what you'll
get. For what? Believe me, my friend—it's not worth
it—"

"You got real money—I know you do!" Mike shouted.
He could feel the panic spreading. His hands were shaking so badly he thought he'd drop the gun. "You cash
payroll checks, you gotta have money t' cash checks—"

"But that's just it," the old man said calmly. "I been
cashing checks all day. Now, money I ain't got . . . I got
a lot of cashed checks. . . . Listen to me," the old man
went on, "leave now, go on, get out of here. You won't
be in any trouble. We'll forget the whole thing. . . ."

Mike hesitated. Maybe the old man was right, maybe
it would—

"Don't let this old son of a bitch bullshit you," Jerry
shouted as he vaulted over the counter and gave the old
man a hard shove backward into the glass shelves behind
him. The old man hit the shelves with a painful grunt,
smashing them, then slid to the floor beneath a shower
of broken bottles. Jerry grabbed one of the broken wine
bottles by its neck and, straddling the old man's chest,
shoved the jagged edge at his face. "Look, you old Jew-
bastard," he shouted viciously through gritted teeth,
"you got about ten seconds to tell us where that money
is or I cut ya face into hamburger. . . ."

The old man raised a shaking finger, pointing to the
cash register, which contained thirty-six dollars, counting change.

"Where's the rest of it?" Jerry screamed. "I can't buy
shit with this." He came at the old man again. "Come up
with the rest of it, you kike bastard," he shouted, grab-

bing the old man's shirt, "or you gonna die—like right now—"

"That's enough," Mike yelled, grabbing Jerry's arm and pulling him off the old man, then dragging him around the counter and toward the door. "Come on, damn it, let's just get our asses outa here."

Mike managed to get Jerry out of the liquor store and into the car in spite of his bitching and shouting about how he wanted to go back in and kill that old bastard.

Neither of them saw Old Man Kellerman as he managed to reach under the counter by the cash register and press the silent alarm button.

They were speeding down Colorado Boulevard when they first heard the siren, and Mike saw the flashing red light coming up fast behind them.

He slammed the accelerator pedal to the floor, at the same time making a quick right on Verdugo Road. The police car stayed with them, closing fast. Mike made a squealing left on Broadway, then opened the Chevrolet up. He was doing ninety before he saw the roadblocks and police cars across the highway three blocks ahead of them. He glanced in the rearview mirror. The police car was gaining on them, now only about two blocks behind.

Mike fought the impulse to slam on the brakes. Behind the cops, the wooden barriers stood like an immovable wall across the center of the highway, less than a block ahead of him. He knew he couldn't stop—he didn't dare. If he stopped they'd be caught and put in a jail cell, and he'd spent eight of the last twelve years in one jail or another. He swore he'd die before he'd let himself be put in another ten-by-twelve. He glanced at Jerry slouched on the seat beside him. The creep was sitting with both arms tightly hugging his stomach, as if he had cramps. His face was chalk-white and bathed in sweat, his eyes were wide and fixed straight ahead. Mike wondered how he'd ever teamed up with a creepy bastard like this. . . .

"Brace yourself, turkey," Mike told him. "We're bustin' through."

They were doing seventy-five when they hit the wooden barriers. There was a hard crashing jolt, and splintered wood flew in all directions. One large piece of two-by-four smashed into the center of the windshield, shattering it and sending an explosion of jagged glass fragments throughout the interior of the car, but somehow only a few small splinters caught Mike in the right cheek and neck as he covered his eyes with his arm and turned his face away. It did, however, cause him to momentarily lose control of the car, which sideswiped two parked cars before he could straighten the wheel, then floor the accelerator and take off down the deserted street leaving a steady stream of water from the ruptured radiator, his front right wheel, knocked out of alignment by the collision, squealing and wobbling in protest.

Jerry finally straightened up in the seat. He had a deep gash on his forehead, which he seemed not even to notice. He looked around wide-eyed as they sped down the deserted street. "Jeez . . . do you know where the hell we are? I think this is where those damn killer spiders are supposed to be—"

"Would you rather spend your life in the can? Anyhow, most of what you heard is bullshit. You don't see any spiders, do you?"

"Then how come the cops ain't followin' us?" Jerry asked, looking behind them.

Mike had no answer.

They continued down Broadway, then Mike made a screeching right on Brand Avenue and floored the accelerator again. Except for an occasional streetlight the boulevards and cross-streets were cast in a shadowy darkness. No lights burned in stores or houses—or anywhere at all along the deserted streets.

"Hey, man," Jerry said, gripping the door handle tightly to keep from bouncing all over the seat, "you can slow down now. Ain't nobody chasin' us now. We're cool."

"I ain't gonna feel cool till we're outa this area," Mike answered nervously.

"Yeah . . . well, that front wheel sounds like it's gonna fly off 'bout any minute, an' the radiator's steamin' like a son of a bitch."

"I don't care," Mike said. "Car's fucked anyway." He stepped harder on the accelerator to emphasize the point. He'd just made a quick right turn on Lexington Boulevard and they were picking up speed again . . . when the street in front of them erupted with a flowing mass of huge black spiders, pouring up out of the sewer grates on both sides of the street, spreading out in all directions, converging in the center of the highway like a moving flood of black tar.

Mike instinctively cut the wheel sharply to the left, trying to avoid the advancing sea of spiders flowing into the street thirty yards in front of them. The car veered sharply to the left and jumped the curb, then went crashing out of control through the plateglass window of a sporting goods store. Mike, frozen with panic, kept the accelerator pressed to the floor. The car roared through the store, shattering showcases and knocking over displays until it collided with the back wall of the store. The impact sprang the car door, sending Mike flying sideways through the air, then sliding across the tile floor until he smacked solidly into the far wall. Jerry was thrown forward through the jagged opening in the windshield, then back against the seat again, where he lay crumpled, the deep gashes in his chest and stomach spurting blood.

Mike lay stunned against the wall, blinking his eyes

rapidly to keep from losing consciousness. His left arm and shoulder felt numb. After a moment he tried to sit up, but agonizing pain in both knees stopped him and he fell back onto his face. From the searing pain he felt running down from his knees he knew his legs were broken.

He heard a series of scraping, scratching noises that his numbed brain couldn't identify. He turned his head to look.

A flowing mass of black spiders was scrambling through the jagged opening in the plateglass window, was quickly advancing across the tile floor, straight toward him.

Mike had time for only one terrified, incredulous scream.

IN AN alley leading off Lexington Boulevard Sam moved restlessly. The sound of the Chevrolet smashing through the storefront had awakened him out of his stupor. He pulled himself into a sitting position by leaning against some garbage cans near him, upsetting one of them into his lap. He looked around through bleary eyes. From inside his filthy coat he produced what was left of a bottle of wine, uncapped it and drank thirstily. He returned the near-empty bottle to the inside of his coat, then wiped his mouth on a grimy sleeve. With most of a quart of wine inside him, he felt just fine, lying among the garbage cans in the alley. . . .

He vaguely heard scuffling noises, and turned his watery eyes to look up the alley. There seemed, to be a million large horrible-looking spiders pouring into the mouth of the alley, coming straight at him. He rubbed his eyes and looked again . . . they were still there, still coming. . . .

"Lousy damn cheap wine," he mumbled, taking the

almost empty bottle out of his coat and throwing it against the brick wall. He rolled over on the ground and covered himself with some old newspapers, then closed his eyes for the last time in his life.

"RUN, MY god, run," McNeal shouted as the spiders poured up into the street around them. "Get into the cars, close the windows. . . ."

Police scattered in all directions, slid, scrambled into their cars, slamming doors behind them, then sat helplessly and looked out the windows in disbelief at a street alive with crawling death.

They were everywhere, covering everything. They spread out across sidewalks, covering lawns, even venturing up the sides of buildings. They were hunting, converging on and attacking anything that moved. A styrofoam coffee cup rolled in the middle of the street, perforated with thousands of tiny holes.

McNeal got on the radio, contacted Bryson, gave a quick description of the situation. He also explained the incident with the 2-11 suspects in the Chevrolet and his belief they couldn't possibly have survived the surfacing of those murderous spiders. He'd heard the crash, seen smoke from the fire it must have caused. The fire would probably burn down half the neighborhood before it was dawn, when the spiders would go underground again and the fire department could try to put it out.

"Any casualties?" Bryson asked.

"Not that we know of. There're still probably people in the area—derelicts, would-be looters that hid out during the evacuation. There's nothing we can do about them, they're probably dead by now. . . . What's the deal around your way?"

"Everything's clear in this area," Bryson said. "It seems when they come out, they come out in a mass and limit themselves to a specific area. I don't think we'll have to worry about this part of the city tonight." He checked out his map. "If they stay in your section, they're still well within the evacuated area."

"Then we're getting the hell out of here," McNeal said. "I'll move my units to the outskirts of the area and concentrate on sealing the perimeter."

"Good idea. I'll send six units to help you. Meantime, I'll contact the FCC to make sure all local radio and TV stations carry an emergency bulletin every ten minutes telling people to stay out of the Glendale area."

McNeal contacted the other units in his area. He deployed each police car to a different sector; the populated areas surrounding the perimeter had to be covered by at least one car. The areas had to be covered block by block, the people informed of the possible danger. They would then stop at predetermined locations around the perimeter and assist in keeping the streets blocked.

McNeal started his engine and moved forward. He had to go slowly in order to maintain traction as his tires rolled over the bodies of the spiders. He glanced at his watch, 3:45; dawn would come in another two hours, and they'd again go underground, their night of hunting at an end. From what he could see, stray dogs and cats were the only victims of the spiders. As he drove, he counted sixteen shriveled carcasses, and dozens of cats either crouching on roofs of houses or hanging by their claws from trees and telephone poles.

He looked out at the moving carpet of spiders invading and inspecting everything in their path. If they came upon anything that seemed like food they converged on it like an immense school of piranha, grabbing and tearing and biting at it. . . . He thought of the poison fog they were to use later that morning, hoped to god it would do the job. . . .

151

As he crossed the perimeter and entered the populated section, he switched his radio to PUBLIC ADDRESS. Holding the mike in his right hand, he drove slowly up and down the streets, at frequent intervals announcing, "This is the police, a state of danger exists, stay in your homes, close and lock all doors and windows, under no circumstances leave your homes . . ." his voice echoing off the buildings around him. In the background he could hear the same warning being transmitted by other units in other areas. It would be impossible for anyone within ten square miles not to have heard the warning.

After returning to the perimeter McNeal spent the next two hours in a state of increasing anger and frustration. Situations before had always been cut and dried. If a problem arose, solve it. If a decision had to be made, make it. He just couldn't take what he'd seen in that evacuated area—death, hunting for victims, and he powerless to stop it. . . .

He got Bryson on the radio. "You gonna be at the riverbed later?"

"Yes, I've been assigned to help supervise the operation—"

"Have you picked the men to place the canisters?"

"No, not yet. I'll need two—"

"You'll only need one now," McNeal told him.

"Come on, buddy, you're too old to play hero—"

"Hero, my ass . . . I'm just mad . . . mad as hell. . . ."

Chapter 14

THE GRAY light of dawn filtered through the closed venetian blinds in the main laboratory, giving the large room a cold, dingy appearance. In the small room adjacent to the lab where the test animals were kept, the white rats and guinea pigs lay curled in furry little balls on their beds of wood shavings. Soon they would be squeaking and clamoring to be fed but now they were still curled in sleep, content with their existence.

In the vivariums, the tarantulas slowly moved about, reinspecting their confines, or occasionally testing the glass walls. One of the larger spiders stretched its length up the side of the enclosure, pushing gently on the steel-meshed top. Other tarantuals had tried to burrow in the soft soil, but could only dig down an inch or two before they hit bottom. The dish of water that Dr. Benjamin had placed in each of the enclosures was gone, and now they were searching their confines, looking for food.

There were noises in the hall outside the lab, then the rattle of keys as one was inserted into the door. The double doors swung open, and Johnnie came in, pushing his cleaning cart in front of him. He flipped the switch on the wall, and the entire laboratory was illuminated by the overhead lights.

The tarantulas immediately became active.

After being invited out of the lab last night, and being unable to do his cleaning, Johnnie had taken the elevator down to the basement storeroom, where he sat for a while grumbling and feeling sorry for himself. After drinking up half his bottle of Early Times, he had fallen asleep on an old cot he kept down there for just that purpose; there were many evenings when he was either too tired, or had gotten too drunk, to make the trip by bus into East Los Angeles, where he lived.

He was glad the professor was gone. He knew Dr. Benjamin didn't like him at all and would probably use any excuse he could find to have him fired. He had been janitor in the science building for more than nine years, and he liked his job very much. No one ever rushed him, and he had plenty of time to work slowly and take it easy; no one was ever around to bother him when he worked late at night. Everyone seemed to like him except Dr. Benjamin. This only meant he had to be very careful when he cleaned on the sixth floor. . . .

Johnnie looked around the lab; everything was in its place and standing neatly. He wouldn't have too much to do in here, maybe just empty the waste baskets and mop the floor. He saw the tarantulas lined up along the glass of their tanks, and went over to have a closer look.

"You sure are ugly mothers," he said, peering at them in fascination. He had never seen spiders that large before. "I'd sure hate to find one of you settin' under my bed grinnin' at me."

One of the tarantulas poised, then struck at the glass, startling him.

"Holy God," he mumbled, jumping backward. "You're mean, too. I'd sure hate to tangle with you."

The spiders had, not unreasonably, scared Johnnie, who did exactly what he had always done when something scared or confused him . . . he turned his back and tried to ignore them. He checked the wastepaper baskets; only one of them had anything in it. He emptied the basket into a plastic bag attached to the side of the cleaning cart. Then he poured a soap-and-ammonia solution onto the floor and began mopping.

He had mopped most of the laboratory floor and was backing down one of the front aisles, moving the mop in even, back-and-forth swirls in front of him. Behind him, he could hear the tarantulas' increased activity as he neared them. They were really making him nervous. Leaning his mop against the edge of a table, he went over to the cleaning cart and dug out his bottle of Early Times. He uncapped it and took two long pulls, capped it and replaced the bottle carefully under the pile of rags. Just one more aisle, he thought nervously to himself, then I'll be finished and I can get the hell outa here. . . . As he reached the end of the aisle, moving the mop as quickly as he could, the mophead tangled around one of the metal legs of a lab table, the cords getting wedged underneath. He pulled on the mop; the cords only wedged tighter. He pulled again—no use, it was stuck. The table was eighteen feet long and weighed several hundred pounds, too heavy for him to lift or move. He ran his fingers through his graying, wiry hair and surveyed the situation. Only one way to free the damn thing. Pull hard . . .

He gripped the mop handle firmly in both hands down near the head and with a grunt pulled with all his strength. The tangled cords tore and broke free under the pressure, and the mop came loose.

Johnnie staggered backward a few steps with the momentum of his effort, the handle of the mop striking the glass face of one of the vivariums, smashing it. He regained his balance, stood for a moment staring wide-eyed at the smashed enclosure and the two mangled tarantulas. "Oh . . . oh my god," he said, slowly shaking his head. "Now I'm really gonna git it. . . ."

He could clearly picture in his mind what the professor would say and do when he discovered what had happened. He'd sure be fired, maybe even go to jail, which thoughts scared the hell out of Johnnie.

He gathered up whatever cleaning utensils he had taken out, threw the mop on top of the cleaning cart and wheeled it all quickly out the doors. He came back into the lab, looked around for anything out of place. Everything looked pretty much as he'd found it, maybe no one would even know he was here. If Dr. Benjamin asked him what had happened he'd lie and say he didn't know— deny everything. After all, it would be his word against . . . nobody's; no one had been here to see what happened. He went out again, closing and locking the double glass doors behind him.

After a few moments of immobility, the tarantulas cautiously inspected the jagged hole in the glass. Then, one by one, they crept out through the hole and crawled across the table.

MCNEAL APPROACHED the access road leading down to the floor of the Los Angeles riverbed. Below him he could see a number of police cars and fire trucks parked in a large semicircle in front of one of the concrete openings to the underground drainage tunnels. There was also cluster of official-looking black limousines parked a short distance away. He recognized Bryson's car standing near a white van off to the side. Bryson was the man he wanted to talk to.

With the first dull rays of the rising sun, the spider mass had gone underground, their night of hunting at an end. Driving through the evacuated area, heading toward the riverbed, McNeal had seen them pouring into the drainage inlets at every streetcorner he had passed. He watched them as they disappeared underground. But were they all going? How many of them still remained in the houses and buildings? Whether what he suspected was true or not, he was sure that section of the city would not be habitable for some time to come.

He drove down the access road and across the dry riverbed, parked near the always-present television van and hoisted himself out of the car. He had to steady himself against the side of the car as a brief wave of dizziness hit him. The last forty-eight hours of tension and strain, together with almost no sleep, were taking their toll. His eyes burned, and his eyelids felt like sandpaper. He also had the beginning of what was sure to be a king-size headache. He leaned back against the car and closed his eyes for a moment, then took several deep breaths, hoping to revive himself.

BRYSON WAS in the process of disagreeing with Mayor Bradshaw and Chief Richardson when he saw McNeal drive up and park. He felt they were all making a serious mistake, putting emphasis on the placing and using of

157

the poison fog canisters to the exclusion of all other possibilities. If the fog proved unsuccessful, he said, they'd be even worse off than now because of the loss of time.

"Captain," Chief Richardson said, "we will continue as planned, in the manner stated, at the time stated. Clear?"

Bryson nodded, without letting anyone think he'd changed his mind. . . . Now he saw McNeal trudging slowly toward them. He grimaced; now would come the argument. This was something he was definitely not looking forward to, mainly because if McNeal's argument was strong enough, he'd be forced to do something he didn't want to do.

As McNeal came up, Bryson could tell by the stern set expression on his face that he definitely had trouble on his mind. He decided to let him get whatever it was off his chest before they had any discussion about whether or not he'd be allowed to volunteer. McNeal's wanting to volunteer to go into the tunnels with the canisters had startled him. He knew McNeal to be a conscientious, dedicated man, but this seemed to be something more, something deeper. He'd tried briefly to talk him out of it when he'd mentioned volunteering over the radio. No go.

Bryson checked his watch. They weren't scheduled to begin the thing for at least another hour. He'd have time to talk it over with McNeal, then make his decision. . . .

McNeal approached the group and asked the mayor if he'd requested the National Guard. Mayor Bradshaw told him he had, and that the governor, at his request, had put the Guard on twenty-four hour alert in case they were needed—

"They're needed right now," McNeal said. "They

should be moved into the Glendale area, along with every police officer we can spare. They've got to be armed with insecticide and dressed protectively. They've got to search every house and building—"

"Lieutenant, slow down," Chief Richardson said. "We haven't the slightest idea what the hell you're talking about."

McNeal took a deep breath, then gave them a quick description of everything that had occurred that morning. He ended by explaining, through firsthand knowledge, the kind of construction used in the old houses and buildings in the area and his personal feelings about the potential danger.

Mayor Bradshaw led him over to two men in business suits conferring with Drs. Perelli and Selby, a Professor Meyers and Professor Winkler from the Smithsonian Institution in Washington, D.C., who'd flown in late the night before to help out any way they could. "Please explain, lieutenant, what you've just told us."

When McNeal had finished, Professor Meyers said, "I think we can now fully appreciate the hypothesis given us by Dr. Benjamin and Dr. Selby . . . these mygalomorphs in their mutant state are without a doubt a tremendous threat."

Professor Winkler nodded. "Lieutenant, your estimate of the probable threat these creatures present is certainly correct, but we won't bother ourselves too much with the possibility of their remaining in the buildings. That would be highly unlikely—"

"How can you be so sure?"

"These creatures," Dr. Perelli put in, "seem to be extremely colonistic by instinct. They hunt at night in a mass colony and will return again to wherever the colony has made its home. From what we've learned the colony has few if any stud males and loners; they all exist as one large, extremely close-knit group. . . . Still"—and he turned now to the mayor—"I would advise you to take the lieutenant's suggestion in any case. You must seek out and destroy them. I warn you, though, these tarantulas cut off from the main colony for any reason will be disoriented and extremely aggressive and dangerous. They need to be handled with extreme care."

"We've already widened the perimeter around the evacuated area three times," Bryson said. "None of those officers can be spared for a search. If anything, we should try to get them a relief shift. Most of them have been on duty for fourteen hours, or more."

The Mayor used the mobile telephone in his limousine to order the National Guard, under the supervision of officials from the health department, into the Glendale area for a building-by-building search and destroy of whatever spiders remained.

A large white panel truck with the insignia of the department of city engineers decaled on both cab doors came rumbling down the access road and across the dry riverbed. It drove past the site where the television crews were setting up their mobile cameras, and parked by the cluster of police cars. This was the truck delivering the poison fog canisters.

McNeal caught Bryson's eye and they exchanged a look they both understood. McNeal raised an inquisitive eyebrow.

Bryson took McNeal's arm. "George, come over here where we can talk. . . . I'm not going to let you do it—"

"I want to, Frank, and why not? I'm as qualified as anyone else you could get—more so, considering I've been involved in this thing right from the beginning. You know I can handle it—"

"Do I? George, you're no youngster anymore—and maybe just a touch overweight. Anyway, you're in no shape to go running around in the tunnels with a hundred and fifty pounds of equipment on your back."

"Look, I'll never know if I had anything to do with this whole thing getting started, or if I could have done something to prevent it. At least I can be in on the finish. I've *got* to go."

Bryson looked at McNeal for a long moment. "All right, George," he finally said, "if it's that important to you, you just volunteered." He gave McNeal a disgusted look. "Come on, we've got to get suited up."

"What do you mean, 'we'?"

Bryson gave him a sour look. "I mean, dummy, you and me. . . ."

DR. BENJAMIN stepped out of the elevator and started down the hall to the science lab.

He was annoyed that after an all too lengthy meeting with Dr. Perelli and those two entomologists—he couldn't even remember their names—Christine had allowed herself to be talked into going with them out to the riverbed as another technical adviser while the police tried the Cloredine gas. He'd said that in his opinion the Cloredine wouldn't be effective and had urged her not to waste valuable time by going . . . after all, the bacteriological notion was hers . . . but after hearing their argument she'd agreed to go anyway, reminding him that it was still only theory. So it was left that he would do the preliminary slide workups on the bacteriological cultures alone and she would be at the lab as soon as she could get back to help with the rest of the tests.

It had become obvious from the start that the others doubted their findings and the talks had ended with the entomologists asking to come to the lab later that afternoon to begin tests of their own . . . or, more accurately, to repeat the tests he and Christine had already done to corroborate—or discredit—their theories. Well, in a way he couldn't blame them . . . the facts and theories they'd been told *were* a little hard to swallow. . . .

He unlocked the doors to the main lab and went in, locking them behind him. He began removing his jacket to replace it with a clean lab coat when an almost tangible sense of foreboding struck him—his eyes went to the smashed vivarium, and his reaction was instant disbelieving terror—*they were loose.* . . .

He froze where he stood, then he saw them, advancing quickly across the floor from different directions. Toward him.

He spun around, his arms still tangled in his coat sleeves, dug desperately into his trouser pocket for the keys to the door. As his fingertips barely touched the keys he felt a sharp, stinging pain in his right leg. Then another one. He looked down to see a large tarantula clinging to his lower trouser leg, sinking its fangs into the calf of his leg. He staggered backward as his right leg at first had the prickly sesation of a million tiny sharp needles, then felt numb. He collided with a lab table, upsetting beakers and test tubes, knocking books and equipment to the floor as he sprawled across the table. He felt a rush of dizziness, his skin felt clammy. He gripped the edge of the table, straightened up, then felt another stinging pain on his right thigh . . . and just beyond his blurred field of vision he could see the others advancing on him.

He kicked out hard with his right leg, smacking his right calf into the steel leg of the table; a squashed spider dropped off. His right leg felt completely numbed as he hobbled down the length of the table, using its edge for support. He knew he had to keep moving. . . . He tried pulling the clinging spider off his thigh but it held on, digging in deeper. He could feel the pressure of the fangs and claws, but could no longer feel the pain.

Maneuvering himself down to the opposite end of the table where his surgical equipment lay, he grabbed a long scalpel and jabbed it through the spider's thorax and into the fleshy part of his thigh. Wincing with pain, he withdrew the scalpel; the spider spasmed and twitched, but hung on. He jabbed again; this time the scalpel came away with an impaled tarantula on it. He threw the scalpel across the room, where it hit a blackboard and fell to the floor, the impaled tarantula still twitching spasmodically.

Beads of sweat stood out on his face, and the laboratory around him began spinning dizzily. The white spots flashing before his eyes told him he was fading into unconsciousness. He could *not* let that happen . . . he had to hold on . . . his life depended on it. . . . He shook his head in an effort to clear it, then began gulping deep breaths of air—it helped, his vision cleared some. His right leg began stinging and burning terribly, the numbness beginning to wear off. Blood ran freely from the open wounds in his thigh, staining his pant leg and dripping onto the floor.

He felt something move on his left shoe. He quickly shook and kicked his foot, sending a spider skidding across the floor. He saw another one standing motionless, feeding on a small pool of his blood. He stamped it into a pulp.

This was insane . . . he was literally fighting for his life against, for god's sake, *spiders*. . . . He saw another one closing on him across the floor. Taking a step forward, he squashed it under the heel of his shoe. . . . How many more were there? He couldn't remember. He glanced around. Two were mangled and obviously dead in the smashed enclosure—three, no, four, he had killed himself. He was sure that that was the enclosure he had taken his dissection specimens from—which would have left eight. He saw what he thought were the remaining two coming toward him down the aisle between the tables. As they approached he managed to kill them too.

The dizziness was returning, worse than before. He took off his coat and put it across a chair, loosened his tie and unbuttoned his shirt collar. He felt extremely lightheaded, his vision was blurring again. He leaned forward and braced both hands against the table in front of him to support his weight as his right leg and thigh began aching and throbbing—he caught only a quick movement out of the corner of his eye as a huge tarantula darted out from behind a clutter of books and viciously attacked his left forearm. He pulled his arm back, shook it violently, a sound of revulsion and surprise escaping his lips. Spider venom, in the form of a hard knot of excruciating pain, traveled quickly up his arm. When it reached his shoulder, he cried out in agony and banged his forearm down on the tabletop as hard as he could, then banged it again and again, but the spider, large enough to wrap its legs completely around his arm, took the blows and hung on tighter than ever.

The pain was unbearable; the spider's claws, after shredding his shirt sleeve, were slicing and gouging his arm, its long fangs repeatedly sinking into the soft flesh. Blood spurted and ran into his clenched fist as a wrist artery was severed.

He began to scream, pain and panic becoming too much for him. Throwing his right arm across his eyes, he staggered down the aisle between the tables, wildly swinging his tortured left arm in front of him, smacking and banging it into anything that was in his way. Books went flying, instruments crashed to the floor, his gas chamber hit the wall and splintered into a million pieces.

His thrashing arm finally collided with the rack of bacteriological cultures, sending the glass vials smashing and breaking against walls and floor.

His left arm was numbed, as much from the beating it had taken as from the spider's deadening venom. His shoulder ached with an agony he'd never experienced and he was near exhaustion; still, the spider held on. Then, one rational thought made its way through the pain and fear—acid. . . . He stumbled and staggered but managed to make his way to the steel-and-glass cabinet on the wall over the sink. Without hesitation, he put his left fist through the glass door, smashing the entire panel out. He withdrew his hand; his knuckles were cut and bleeding.

It was becoming more and more difficult for him to move his arms and legs; it was as though he had lost all control over them. He found it increasingly difficult to concentrate on a clear thought—as if he were detached from his body, as if his mind was off to one side, observing his body going through the motions. But a conscious point still heard the frantic banging on the laboratory doors, and people shouting his name. But it all seemed so distant, and unfamiliar. . . .

Summoning all that was left of his ability to concentrate, he managed to find the glass bottle he needed, a 50% solution of sulfuric acid. He got out the glass stopper and, carefully as he could, poured some over the spider still clinging to his arm. The spider twitched and jerked, a wispy white, foul-smelling vapor rising from its back. Finally, after what seemed a lifetime, the spider dropped off into the sink.

He felt for the water tap and turned it on, then plunged his tortured left arm under the flow. His vision was a blurred mass of swirling colors, his mind completely disoriented. He could no longer stand on his feet. He took three stifflegged steps away from the sink, then dropped to the floor. Unconscious.

MCNEAL TRIED taking a deep breath, groaned with discomfort. "It's no use," he said, shaking his head miserably. "I can't breathe in this damned thing. It's too tight, and I'm just too fat."

"If you'd loosen those two adjustment straps across your back a little more," Bryson suggested, walking over to his friend, "and the two holding the air tank maybe you wouldn't feel like some kind of space sausage." He made the necessary adjustments to McNeal's protective flame suit.

McNeal nodded and tried walking around again in the cumbersome suit. Its only flexibility was in an elastic tuck-and-roll effect at each of the body joints—elbows, knees and such—it was like trying to move about in a body-length straitjacket. To make matters worse, it was still unbelievably tight, pinching and cutting into him under his arms, and especially in his crotch. He was miserable.

Bryson, as always, looked cool, seemingly moving about with ease in his own heavy, bulky suit. McNeal eyed him with a look of disdain. "I don't know how the hell you do it," he said disgustedly.

"Do what?"

"Well, goddamn it, we've both been on duty for"— McNeal glanced at his watch, which was lying on the back seat of the police car along with his coat and other articles from his pockets—"almost fifty hours straight. I admit it—I'm tired. I haven't eaten—I have a tension headache—I need sleep—goddamn it, I'm beat!" He gave Bryson a distasteful look. "But, you . . . look at you. Fresh as a damned daisy. You look like you just got off a two-week vacation."

Bryson just grinned at him.

"Come on, admit it, damn you. You're on uppers, aren't you? Some kind of amphetamines, right?" McNeal looked at him suspiciously.

"George," Bryson said, his face turning serious. "I'm not taking pills. I guarantee you, I'm as beat as you are. . . . I don't know, maybe I've just learned to adjust, or cope with this thing better, though I doubt it. Or maybe" —he patted McNeal's ample belly—"maybe it's that I'm not carrying around the same load you are."

A newscaster approached McNeal before he could reach for an answer. He was followed by a technician carrying a minicamera on his shoulder.

"Hello, I'm John Otis, KNBC news. Lieutenant, exactly what steps are being taken to rid the city of this menace?"

McNeal glanced at Bryson, who had trouble looking him squarely in the eye. He felt like saying the city was using the most dangerous weapons at their disposal, Bryson and himself. Playing it straight, he said, "We'll be going into the tunnel system to place canisters of poison gas."

"Did you two volunteer for this?"

He nodded and tried to move away.

"Why?" the reporter persisted.

But McNeal had had enough of this circus and walked away to join Bryson with the two men at the panel truck.

"Each of these canisters," the older of the two men explained, "has a capacity of about four hundred cubic yards of poison vapor. The canisters should be placed in the tunnels no more than thirty-five yards apart for maximum effectiveness. Now, this," he said, pointing to a red plastic cap with a small wire antenna protruding from its top, "is the radio wave triggering device. We've doubts about whether they'll work properly inside those concrete tunnels—concrete restricts radio waves, you know." He went to the front of the truck and came back with what looked like two small hearing aids. "We'll be in direct contact with you through these miniature transceivers. They fit in and around the ear, held in place by this wire clip. You can also communicate with each other through them. When they're in place, you only have to talk." He went back to the canisters. "If we can't trigger these devices automatically from out here, you'll have to do it manually by pulling straight up on the triggering device and removing it, then slipping out this manual trigger retaining pin located here," he said, pointing to its location, "then just squeeze the trigger."

The vehicle that would transport them into the tunnels was about the size of a golf cart and had an extended tool rack mounted directly behind the bench seat. It was powered by an electric motor supplied by two enormous storage batteries placed directly under the tool rack. It had extra wide, deeply ribbed tires, and a wide sheet-metal skirt that had been added on. The skirt stood straight out from the body of the small car, completely encircling it; its obvious function was to repel the spiders, keep them from boarding the car.

Time. They fitted their hooded headgear into place, closing the zipper by drawing it in an almost complete circle around their necks, then fastened the snaps that held the draping hood down across their back and shoulders.

No sooner had the headgear been fitted onto the body of McNeal's suit, sealing it, then it became impossible for him to breathe, and he told them so, his voice muffled by the almost airtight material.

The younger of the two technicians immediately went behind McNeal and Bryson and adjusted the metering valve on their air tanks. The suits filled with compressed air and billowed out slightly, the air hiss almost unnoticeable. It also helped to relieve the painful tightness of McNeal's suit, for which he was silently grateful.

"Let's test the transceivers," the older technician said, switching on a radio amplifier mounted in a console in the rear of the van. He spoke to them through a small hand mike.

"Coming in loud and clear," McNeal said, hearing the technician's voice crisp and sharp in his left ear. He could also hear Bryson's agreement that it was clear as a bell. Both their voices came through a speaker mounted on the console in the van.

They clambered aboard the electric car, Bryson taking the driver's side because it would be physically easier for him to drive. Instead of a steering wheel, the car had only a single steering stick coming up from the floorboard. "How the hell do you steer this thing?" Bryson asked.

"Move the stick straight forward to go," the younger technician explained. "Move it slightly to the left or right for steering or turning. There's no reverse, but most of the tunnels are eight to ten feet in width and your car has a tight turning radius of six feet. It was especially designed and built for inspecting these storm-drain tunnels, to turn and maneuver inside them. To stop, just release the stick."

Bryson slowly moved the stick forward and the car ambled up the sloping incline toward the mouth of the tunnel at its top speed of five miles per hour. As they entered the tunnel McNeal had the disquieting impression that they were moving into the gaping mouth of some huge carnivorous beast that was about to swallow them up. He couldn't ignore the hard knot of tension in the pit of his stomach; it felt as if he had swallowed a jagged rock. He thought of the last words his wife had said to him almost two days before . . . "George, please be careful, don't take any unnecessary chances." Well, this was necessary, wasn't it? . . .

Sunlight quickly disappeared behind them as they moved deeper into the wide tunnel. Bryson switched on the four headlights mounted at different angles in the front of the vehicle illuminating the passage in front of them for almost fifty yards. There was no movement ahead; this section of the tunnel was completely empty. They continued on, periodically passing under a thin shaft of bright sunlight from the sewer grates above them.

The concrete walls and floor of the tunnel were stained with long streaks of greenish-brown mold and fungus, from stagnant moisture and water residue. Even through their protective suits, the stagnant, moldy odor of the place reached them; it had the suffocatingly strong smell of decaying vegetation.

It was soon after they had passed the first tunnel inter-section that they began hearing the noises . . . low and muffled at first, off in the distance ahead of them, then growing louder and closer . . . the sound of countless tiny nails scraping and clawing at the rough concrete surface.

Suddenly, ahead of them in the sweeping beams of the headlights they could see them. Millions of them, mill-ing, crawling across the floor of the tunnel, up and over the walls, upside down on the ceiling. It was as though the tunnel itself were made of moving black bodies.

Bryson released the stick and they came to an abrupt stop. They both sat and stared for a moment in shocked silence.

"Holy God," McNeal finally said.

"Amen," Bryson agreed.

The multitude of spiders caught in the bright beams from the headlights shifted and accelerated their movement in rising agitation. They bumped into and crawled over each other, then, en masse, began moving down the tunnel toward McNeal and Bryson, their fangs spread, their front legs held high.

Bryson took a deep breath, then let the air out slowly between his teeth. "Well, friend, you ready for this?"

"No," McNeal answered dismally.

"What's going on in there? What's happening?" the technician's voice broke in over the transceiver.

"You wouldn't believe it," Bryson said. He pushed the stick forward, and they moved slowly toward the advancing mass of spiders.

McNeal tensed, unconsciously gritted his teeth, as they reached the first of the spiders. The crunching, squashing sounds were unmistakable over the echoing clatter of claws as the large wheels began rolling over them. McNeal felt a strong sense of satisfaction on hearing it. It was what the bastards deserved. He reached behind him and picked up one of the canisters, swinging it around onto his lap. "Let's get these things planted," he said nervously, looking at the swarming multitude around them, "then get the hell out of here."

Bryson released the stick, the car stopped. The spiders immediately swarmed up over the wheels, clawed and scraped at the sides of the vehicle, but the skirting shield was effective, none of them could get past it.

McNeal held the canister out over the side of the car at arm's length, then dropped it, squashing spiders underneath as the heavy canister hit the floor of the tunnel.

"The first canister is dropped," Bryson said loudly. "Release it."

Silence. Nothing happened.

"Do you read me? Activate the damn canister," Bryson shouted, tension apparent in his voice.

The transceiver crackled loudly with static. The

sounds that came were so distorted and crackly it was impossible to make out words.

And still nothing happened to the canister.

"What the hell do we do now?" McNeal asked, feeling hopeless.

"Keep dropping the canisters," Bryson said, "and hope to hell we can activate them manually on our way back." He pushed the stick forward and they were moving again.

They dropped four more canisters, and had just stopped to drop the fifth when Bryson, waiting for McNeal to complete his task, looked up at the walls of the tunnel. "Oh, my god!" he said slowly.

"What—?" McNeal began as he turned to look where Bryson's gloved finger pointed.

Suspended from the walls and ceiling of that part of the tunnel were literally millions of white, fibrous sacs, each about the size of a tennis ball. They hung everywhere, attached by short cords of silky webs. Many of them had clusters of small, dark spiderlings moving about on them.

"I don't believe it," McNeal said. "We're in some kind of damn nursery."

"Egg sacs!" Bryson said. "Millions of egg sacs! And they're hatching! Good god!"

"This must be the center of the colony. I saw a few of those things while we were moving in but had no idea what the hell they were—till now."

Bryson said nothing. He just went on staring at the egg sacs.

"And this damn fog won't reach more than two feet off the ground," McNeal said. "It won't even reach to the spiders on the walls. At best we can only hope to kill a few thousand of them. . . ." He took the canister he was holding and pulled the triggering device from its top.

With a gloved finger he removed the retaining pin, then depressed the triggering lever, breaking the seal. Using all his strength he threw the canister out in a flat arc in front of the car. It bounced once, then rolled a short way, sending out a billowing trail of thick, grayish-blue fog.

As the spiders came in contact with the spreading vapor they immediately curled and lay motionless. Many were caught by the fog, but more of them managed to avoid it by crawling quickly up the walls of the tunnel and over the moving bodies of their neighbors.

McNeal and Bryson each threw two more canisters, one straight down the center, one down the left and right walls of the tunnel. By this time the entire floor of the tunnel was covered with a thick blanket of the spreading fog.

"Now," McNeal said, sitting back heavily on the seat, "let's turn this kiddie-car around and get our asses the hell out of here."

They moved forward, Bryson angling the car to within inches of the right wall of the tunnel. He then moved the stick sharply to the left, and they began a tight turn. A little less than three-quarters of the way through the turn, he quickly released the stick; the right front part of the metal skirt was within half an inch of the left tunnel wall. "If I go any further we'll wipe out the skirt."

"Well, we sure as hell can't just sit here," McNeal said, watching as the spiders moved up and filled the space behind them. "We got no choice. *Go.*"

Bryson shoved the stick forward. There was a scraping, crunching sound as the skirt buckled and folded against the concrete wall, then tore completely loose from the right side of the vehicle. The right fender of the Fiberglas body splintered and cracked as it collided with the wall. They still could not complete the turn.

The vibration of their collision brought down a shower

of dislodged spiders into their laps, the spiders crawling over them, clawing and biting at their suits that still effectively protected them.

"The man said we had a six-foot turning radius. I believed him," Bryson said.

"He was wrong," McNeal said dismally. "He didn't figure on the length of the skirt."

"Well, George," Bryson said, "it looks like we've got to walk it home. Take two canisters with you and stick to the center of the tunnel." He brushed spiders off his face shield. "We'll be all right as long as we're in the protection of this fog. After that, we'll use the canisters—without them we'll be drowned in spiders. Jesus . . ."

They lifted themselves out of the vehicle, grabbed two canisters each and started trudging slowly up the tunnel the way they had come.

Even though the trip was slightly downhill, it didn't take McNeal long to begin sweating heavily inside the tight, cumbersome suit; it was with great effort that he could even walk in the thing, much less carry two heavy canisters. After a short while his legs began feeling like lead and his strained breathing fogged the inside of his face shield. In spite of Bryson's urging and encouragement, he had to stop frequently to catch his breath.

The fog was growing thin in the tunnel ahead of them. They stopped long enough to remove the radio control devices and retaining pins from the canisters they carried, then continued on. The floor of the tunnel was littered almost solidly with the curled bodies of the spiders; they crunched and squashed under their boots as they walked. All around them spiders swarmed, and many of them fell to their deaths from the walls and ceiling.

Air currents, coming in from the entrance to the tunnel, were now gently blowing and whipping at the blanket of fog, forcing it past them deeper into the tunnel. Not far ahead McNeal could see the swarming mass of spiders moving safely, unhindered, across the tunnel floor, closing off their avenue of escape.

They now reached the first of the canisters McNeal had dropped and released it. Puffy clouds of thick smoke billowed out and settled along the floor, then were quickly carried down the tunnel—their remaining protection was nearly gone. Up ahead, it seemed like miles away, McNeal could see the small half circle of bright sunlight that was the entrance. They had no other choice but to keep on moving—as long as they could.

McNeal's clothes were soaking wet and pasted to his body. Inside the heavy boots, his feet sloshed, soaked in pools of his own sweat. His hair clung to his face inside the stuffy headgear, and itched like hell. The sweat running in rivulets off his forehead made his eyes burn.

As they stepped out of the protective fringe of fog, the spiders swarmed over them within seconds. Fangs and claws tried, still unsuccessfully, to pierce the fabric of their suits, scratched at their face shields. The weight of the moving bodies on the suits made it almost impossible for the men to walk, even move.

Nonetheless, Bryson managed to bring the canister in his right hand up and between their bodies. He depressed the trigger, and they were immediately engulfed in a smoky cloud of gray fog. Spiders squirmed and clung to them for a few seconds, then dropped off. He held the canister low, then depressed the trigger again and managed to clear a short path for them through the swarming rush of spiders. "Just a little further and we'll be out of here, George," he urged as he pressed the trigger on the second canister.

McNeal said nothing. His head throbbed with his strained blood pressure, and he had a curiously annoy-

175

ing sensation in his left arm . . . sort of a tingling numbness.

The spiders crowded and milled all around them, just
beyond the fringe of the fog Bryson was laying down;
moving with them, following them. There seemed to be
more and more of them, and even more were coming up
from the tunnel intersections behind them.

"Just a little further, George . . . keep moving," and
Bryson used the last of the fog from the third canister.
He couldn't miss McNeal's robot-like movements; could
see his sweat-soaked face through the face shield, the
look of pain in his friend's eyes. He took the fourth, and
last, canister from McNeal, and pressed the trigger.

McNeal's movements were involuntary now, just a
matter of automatically putting one foot in front of the
other. The pulsing pressure in his head was much worse,
it was making him dizzy and lightheaded. His left arm felt
completely numb; he couldn't feel his fingertips against
the rough interior of his gloves any longer. With bright
white spots flashing and dancing in front of his eyes, it
took every bit of his willpower to keep from stumbling
and falling on his face.

Within seconds after the last canister was depleted,
they were overrun and completely covered by clawing,
biting bodies, swarming over them with an almost insane
frenzy, bodies on top of bodies on top of more bodies.

"Keep *moving*, George," Bryson shouted, seeing
McNeal faltering under the terrific weight of the clinging
bodies that covered him. "Don't stop, man, only chance
is to keep moving. . . ."

"I . . . I can't, too much for me," McNeal mumbled
almost incoherently. He stopped in his tracks as a crip-
pling stab of pain tore across the left side of his chest and
down his side. "Frank . . . I can't . . ." was all he could
manage to get out.

176

Bryson turned around to see McNeal drop slowly to his knees, then pitch forward onto his stomach and disappear completely under a living carpet of spiders.

Bryson quickly reached down and got a fistful of the suit's coarse material in each gloved hand, then pulled with all his strength. He could barely move McNeal. "I can't budge you." He pulled again—no use. "Try to get up," he almost pleaded. "Try to get up on your hands and knees, anything. I can't drag you . . . it's impossible. . . ."

Strictly by feel, Bryson located the metering valve on McNeal's air tank and turned it up full. McNeal's suit ballooned out almost to the breaking point before the air began hissing and escaping through the tiny vent holes on each side of the headgear.

The rush of cold air helped. After a few moments McNeal's dizziness and the pounding in his head subsided. He still had the jabs of pain in his chest, but they weren't so bad. Bryson helped him to his feet, at this point completely ignoring the spiders clawing and biting at them. He was just glad they couldn't grip or cling to their face shields or they'd have been blinded by the writhing, moving bodies.

"Lean on me, George," Bryson instructed, getting his shoulder under McNeal's arm.

And supporting McNeal's ponderous weight as best he could, Bryson moved slowly through the seething mass of spiders toward the sunlit entrance to the tunnel.

GROUPS OF policemen and firemen stood by their equipment, intently watching the entrance to the storm-drain system, shading their eyes or squinting in the bright morning sun.

The mayor, Chief Richardson and Dr. Perelli stood by their limousines talking among themselves. Dr. Selby was in deep discussion with the two scientists from the Smithsonian Institution. They all believed that the two officers who'd volunteered to go into the tunnels didn't stand a chance. They were dead. Had to be.

The two technicians were sitting in the back of the white van, still trying to get their radio receiver working again. Why had it quit working? Probably a bad condenser or transistor in the circuit somewhere. They'd thought it was foolproof, never went on the fritz before. . . .

"Look!" one of the firemen was shouting, pointing. "God, look at that!"

Everyone turned to look at the entrance to the drainage system. Two shapes stood in the entrance, so completely encrusted with wriggling, crawling black spiders it was difficult to tell *what* the shapes were. . . .

Bryson, squinting into the bright sunlight, looked at all the staring faces. "We made it, George," he said softly. He gripped McNeal a little tighter under the arm and they started carefully down the enbankment, until knocked off their feet as the spray from a high pressure water hose hit them. They rolled and slid down the concrete embankment, pushed and turned by the spray from the hose. By the time they reached the bottom of the embankment, no spiders clung to them.

Men now ran up to them from all directions as they lay there, stunned. Hands pulled at them, unsnapping their headgear, loosening belts, unzipping zippers. As their headgear was removed, a rush of comparatively cool air washed over their sweat-soaked faces. McNeal took a deep breath, let it out in a long sigh.

Everyone fired questions at them. The mayor and police chief wanted to know if they'd been successful. Dr. Selby and the scientists wanted to hear what they'd observed. The technicians asked what had happened to the

178

canisters and the vehicle. Two teams of paramedics were asking them how they felt. Jesus. Everyone was talking and shouting at once, but a paramedic quickly slipped an oxygen mask over McNeal's nose and mouth before he could even try to respond.

Then while the paramedics loaded McNeal into a waiting ambulance to take him to County General Hospital for a full examination, Bryson answered questions as best he could. "Those things are breeding like crazy in there, and I can't see any way to stop them," he said, looking at Dr. Selby and the professors.

"Millions of egg sacs?" Professor Meyers said, a note of disbelief in his voice. "Are you sure they were egg sacs?"

"I'm sure," Bryson said firmly. "We saw them scattered all through the tunnel, then that big concentration of them in what I assume was the center of the colony. We even saw the baby spiders crawling all over them. They're all hatching."

"But Dr. Benjamin estimated their breeding cycle at *three months,*" Professor Winkler muttered, looking at the others.

"This accelerated breeding cycle means the colony will at least triple in size within a matter of days," Dr. Selby said. She turned to the mayor. "This fantastic number of baby spiders Captain Bryson is talking about will mature enough to join the colony within a day or two, and that means that although the colony has remained confined to a relatively small area of the tunnels up until now, with these added numbers it will grow too large to survive as a group any longer. At some point soon they *will* break off from the parent colony, spread throughout the tunnel system and begin *new* and *separate* colonies."

The mayor looked like a man suddenly told he had

thirty seconds to live. "You're sure of all this?"

"Yes, I'm afraid I am. . . . We've no more than two days to stop them, before there will be no stopping them. . . ."

The mayor left the group without another word, going to the telephone in his limousine.

"We're at a bad disadvantage," Professor Meyers said. "Everything Winkler and I've learned about these creatures has been secondhand. We need to analyze them firsthand to be of any real help. . . . I suggest Winkler and I meet with Dr. Benjamin at his laboratory right away, examine his specimens and conduct a series of tests—"

Mayor Bradshaw came back to the group then. "I've been in contact with Haskel from Globe-Eastern. He seems pretty sure the ammonia spray he mentioned at our meeting will work. He'll use his own trained personnel but he'll need help from you, Richardson, and from you, Perelli. I'm sure your departments will cooperate—"

"Considering how much the colony has grown I seriously doubt a simple ammonia spray will be effective," Dr. Selby put in.

"Well, I've also talked to MacCandell, who contacted the chemical engineers. If the ammonia spray fails we'll pump cyanide gas into the tunnels . . . after evacuating the whole city. . . ." He shook his head. "I know how drastic that sounds, but what alternative do we have?".

A police car came speeding down the access road and across the dry riverbed, screeching to a stop where the group stood talking.

"Is there a Dr. Christine Selby here?" the young officer asked, getting out of the car.

"I'm Dr. Selby," Christine said, looking at him inquisitively.

"I was told to let you know that Dr. Benjamin has been seriously injured in his laboratory and has been taken to the hospital. He was conscious at the hospital long enough to insist you be told—"

"What . . . what happened? Is he hurt badly?. . ."

"Afraid I don't know. I was just sent to tell you—"

"I'll go immediately. Where? What hospital?"

"Harbor General."

"Can you drive me?" Without waiting for an answer she went around to the passenger side of the car and got in.

The officer got back into his car and they sped off.

After she'd gone Bryson managed to wiggle out of the cumbersome flame suit, told them where he planned to be if they needed him for anything, then quickly left in a police car.

First stop: County General Hospital to see how an overweight cop named McNeal was making out.

Chapter 15

By the mayor's order, the remaining southeastern portion of Glendale, the city of Eagle Rock and the northeastern portion of Highland Park were evacuated. The nervous population was instructed to take only essentials with them, things they could easily carry. They were loaded on city buses and transported wherever possible to families and friends or volunteer homes in other parts of Los Angeles County. By four o'clock that afternoon not a man, woman or child remained in the area. The news media treated the evacuation low-key and carefully, and panic and disorderly incidents were kept to a scattered minimum. All National Guard, Army reserve and police reserve units in the southern California area were activated and quickly moved into the evacuated area, forming a tight cordon of men and equipment around the new perimeter, sealing it completely. Local martial law was applied within the area. Through frequent broadcasts it was made known that unauthorized individuals caught in the area would be subject to arrest, and that vandals and looters would be shot on sight.

After a long, painstaking building-by-building search of the Glendale area, health department officials had turned in a grisly report: They had discovered the shriveled, mummified remains of twenty-three people, all of whom were assumed to be looters, in and around houses and buildings heavily infested with spiders. The infested houses and buildings were fumigated with strong pesticides, and in cases where infestation was too heavy the houses and buildings were set on fire and burned to the ground.

The only casualties of the search occurred when three National Guardsmen, searching the attic of a house for spider infestation, found what they were looking for.

By late afternoon the search had been completed, the area cleared and readied for the extermination team with the ammonia spray, and over two hundred more specimens had been delivered to the main laboratory at UCLA.

DR. BENJAMIN rose slowly out of nightmarish delirium, up into the brighter world of semiconsciousness. He was vaguely aware of his surroundings—the clean, white sheet and pillowcase he rested on, the warm comfort of the room. He was aware of people near his bed, could hear the buzz of their conversation though he couldn't make out the words. He opened his eyes but could only

184

see blurred shadows. He tried to move, couldn't. He felt as though his entire body were packed in a thick layer of soft cotton. His mouth felt impossibly dry, as if it too had been stuffed with cotton. He tried to speak but could only manage a low groan. He felt a sharp twinge of pain as a hypodermic needle was inserted into his right arm.

He was drifting again now, down into unconsciousness. The nightmare was returning, getting closer, waiting for him just beneath the surface of the darkness. His mind pulled back—he could see *them* again. He could hear them snarling at him—fanged mouths leering at him with disgusting, malicious grins. They were pulling at him with fangs and claws, ripping at him, tearing out great chunks of flesh, disemboweling him. His mind screamed and fought against them, but they continued pulling him down, deeper into themselves. He could feel them as they swirled and swarmed over his face and head, drawing him deeper, deeper into their ugly darkness. . . .

He felt a finger raise his eyelid, then a bright light being shined into his eye. He turned his head to the side, blinking, then opened both eyes.

"Well, hello," the doctor bending over him said. "I'm Dr. O'Brien. Nice to have you back with us again."

He tried to focus his mind, still cloudy with sleep and drugs. Residue of his nightmarish dream still clung to his subconscious, making it hard for him to distinguish it from reality. He closed his eyes again, concentrated on the doctor's voice.

"Now, just relax, take it slow. You'll probably still be a little woozy from the tranquilizer I gave you. You should feel better in a while." He examined his pupils again.

"What . . . what happened to me? How long have I . . . was I . . .?"

185

"A student found you. You've suffered some pretty nasty wounds on your left arm and right leg," Dr. O'Brien told him. "We're also treating you for shock and toxic poisoning. That dose of spider venom had quite an effect on your nervous system."

His mind was now clearing, comprehension was returning, and he noticed for the first time his heavily bandaged left arm and the IV tube inserted into his forearm just below the elbow.

"What's the damage to my arm?" he asked, wiggling his fingers, which were visible at the end of the mass of bandages.

"Multiple lacerations of the forearm and wrist. The most damage was to a carotid artery in the lower forearm, just above the wrist. It'll have to remain sutured and bandaged for at least three weeks. Other than that, you appear to be in pretty good condition, all things considered. As massive a dose as that toxic venom was, it seems to have dissipated throughout your system, there seem no significant damage or side effects."

Dr. Benjamin's mind was completely clear now, and with the clarity came a nauseating fear. "I'll also require a complete blood and urine analysis," he said, hardly able to keep a slight quiver of nervousness out of his voice, "upper and lower GI series, and a magnified fluoroscope series of the kidneys, liver, spleen and pancreas."

"All right . . . but, why? What are we looking for?"

"Spider eggs," Dr. Benjamin told him, straightfaced.

"Sp—you can't be serious."

"I'm afraid I am."

"Well, of course, we'll do as you ask, but frankly—"

"I know it sounds farfetched, but let me explain. This species of tarantula is just like nothing we've ever dealt with before. I won't bother you with the particulars. Let me say that this species is more than capable of doing

186

what I suggest. I won't take the chance that they've
. . . infected me. . . ."

"But if that were the case wouldn't the initial blood
analysis show it?"

"Not necessarily," Dr. Benjamin said, not really wanting to talk about it any further. "If the eggs are present,
they're quickly trapped by the various organs—especially the kidneys and spleen. Only a detailed fluoroscope of these organs would show them up."

"I see," the doctor said, without much conviction.
"Well, you'll have to be scheduled for these tests. I'll see
to it immediately. Meantime I'd advise you to rest."

"Doctor, it's important I get out of here as soon as
possible. How long will I be here?"

"Ordinarily I would have considered releasing you by
tomorrow morning, but in light of these extra tests
you're insisting on I would say in two days, if there are
no complications." He went to the door. "Now, try to get
some sleep. I'll be back to you very soon," and he left the
hospital room.

Dr. Benjamin lay back on his pillow and closed his
eyes. He said a silent prayer that his suspicions were
unfounded. Because, if they were true, he knew he was
a dead man.

He heard the door open again, and the rustling sound
of someone entering the room. He opened his eyes as
Christine Selby sat down in the chair by the side of his
bed. She took his hand in hers.

"How do you feel?" she asked softly.

The question seemed to force whatever emotions he
felt to rise to the surface. "I'm scared, Christine, scared
as hell."

"I CAN'T eat this crap," McNeal said irritably, eyeing the
lunch tray containing a runny poached egg, a small bowl

187

of oatmeal, a glass of some kind of yellow juice and two pieces of *dry* toast. "Take this stuff away and get me the doctor. And bring my clothes over here."

"I'm afraid I can't do that," the young nurse said sternly. "The doctor is making his rounds right now. He'll be in to see you soon." She headed for the door.

McNeal didn't like hospitals. He firmly believed that they were invented by the American Medical Association for the express purpose of putting people at their mercy. Once you entered a hospital, the doctors had you, body and soul. They had complete control over the medication and drugs they fed you, they could sit back and see what effect it had on you, they could lay you out on an operating table, and once there, at their own discretion, cut out whatever little old parts of you they felt like. If you didn't happen to live through all of this, it was never their fault; *they* had done everything they could, but *you* were just too far gone to make it—as though dying was an insult to them and a reflection on you. Boy, they literally had it coming and going.

He walked across the cold floor to the closet, his white hospital gown billowing out behind him—another of his favorite peeves. He was positive that hospital gowns were especially designed to afford the maximum of discomfort and embarrassment to the patient wearing them —there was *no* way to wear one without having your ass hanging out the back.

He found his clothes hanging in the closet. They were incredibly dirty, but at least he could wear them home, then change. He gingerly carried them back to the bed and piled them on the chair. He went back to the closet for his shoes—

There was a soft knock on the door, it opened and his wife came in carrying a large paper bag and a small valise. She looked first to the bed, then, seeing he wasn't there, turned around.

"George, why aren't you in bed? You shouldn't be up walking around."

He came over and put his arms around her, gave her a kiss. "I'm feeling great, Doris. The electrocardiogram was normal, so there's nothing wrong with my heart. My blood pressure was up but the doctor said it was all due to extreme strain and fatigue. He said I should just take it sort of easy for the next few days and get some rest. Well, I can do that at home. With you. I'll let Frank carry the ball for a day or so. . . . Hell, rank has its privileges, right?"

"Well," she said doubtfully, "if you really promise." She placed the bag and the valise on the bed. "I brought you clean clothes to wear. I think we'll take those home and burn them," she said, making a sour face at the pile of clothes draped across the chair. She opened the valise and took out a fresh suit, a clean shirt, socks and under-wear.

McNeal had just finished dressing when the doctor came in. "Well, you're certainly not wasting any time getting back on your feet, are you? . . . Lieutenant, I don't think you quite realize what's happened to you. It was a warning—a serious warning. You need to stop working as strenuously as you have, watch your diet carefully, and above all let your body rest and recuperate. If you don't you're in for serious trouble, I promise you."

McNeal assured him he understood, but that there were some things to be done and—

"Lieutenant, you're fifty-two, you weigh two hundred and sixty-three pounds. What you say you've had to do the last few days would probably put too much strain on a man half your age, and a hundred pounds lighter."

"I know—"

"Listen to me." He looked at McNeal's chart. "When you were brought into emergency, your blood pressure was one-ninety over one-forty. That's too much strain for your heart. It works hard enough thanks to the excessive weight you're carrying around—"

"I intend to spend at least a couple of days lying flat on my back, taking it easy. I'll watch my diet too. I know I eat like a horse," McNeal said sheepishly.

"As far as your diet is concerned, it's not how much you eat as what. Oh, you've definitely got to lose some of that weight, but at the moment I want you to concentrate on a salt-free, low-cholesterol diet. And above all avoid any strenuous activity."

"Well, I'll certainly try to do that, doc—"

"You must do it. If you don't stay on the diet I prescribe for you, and avoid strenuous activity, I can pretty well guarantee that you'll have a heart attack—and a serious one at that—in the very near future."

McNeal's wife was pale. "Oh, he'll stay on his diet, and follow your recommendations," she said, looking at McNeal almost threateningly. "Won't you, George? You're no good to any of us dead, you know."

"Well, since you put it that way, you have my word on it."

He picked up his valise and they went to the door. "Whatever it is that's going to happen to this city, I guess it's going to happen without the intrepid crime fighter, George McNeal."

By 10:30 that Saturday night over three thousand men were involved in securing and sealing of the perimeter around the newly evacuated area. Men and vehicles had been deployed in an almost shoulder-to-shoulder cordon around the area. When the spiders did finally surface again, they knew they would be powerless to combat

190

them. Their sole objective was to keep people out of the area, out of imminent danger.

The new perimeter gave them a three-mile margin between where the spider mass had surfaced the night before and the edge of the evacuated area. When the spiders did surface, they would almost surely have to surface within that area.

The operation earlier that afternoon had, in a word, been a disaster. Large chemical trucks loaded with ammonia solution were parked at strategic locations around the city. Trained chemical technicians wearing protective clothing had hooked incredibly long spray hoses to the trucks and had taken the hoses down through manholes to spray the tunnels. The spray hoses were later recovered. The technicians were never seen again.

The men stood silently now, staring into the lifeless area, ready at the slightest sign of movement to radio a warning. Conversation was almost nonexistent. The only sounds that could be heard as the men stood nervously at their assigned posts were the constant staticky chatter from the police radio and the weirdly terrifying noises that echoed up from the street beneath their feet. It was not a particularly warm night, but perspiration stood out on the tense faces of most of the men as they stood silently watching.

They knew it would be coming again, rising up out of the street and covering everything in its frantic search for food. What the men didn't know was when, or where.

THE LE Grande movie theater stood on Colorado Boulevard in South Pasadena, a little more than eight miles from the northeastern border of the evacuated area, actually more than twelve miles from the last surfacing of the spider mass. It was an old theater, and for the last twenty years had been a third-rate movie house showing

191

B-features. Recently a large theater chain had purchased the Le Grande and had completely revamped it. The theater now had a new and stylish decor in the main lobby, plush new carpeting throughout, even a new movie screen and draping curtain. The Le Grande was a beautiful new theater, showing nothing but limited engagement first-run films.

At 11:45 the manager of the theater left his office after counting the receipts for the day, came down the stairs into the main lobby and happily told the assistant manager that, even with the threat hanging over the city, they still had an attendance of over six hundred people—more than half the theater's capacity. He told the two girls working behind the candy counter to close it up, alerted the ushers to get ready because the show was scheduled to be let out in twenty minutes. He then went to the entrance of the theater, swung open the glass doors, stood for a moment in the doorway enjoying the cool breeze that rushed in and looking up admiringly at the beautifully flashing marquee.

At 11:50 the street in front of the Le Grande theater erupted with a sea of spiders. They quickly covered the street and sidewalk, then flooded through the open doors into the movie theater.

At 12:00 midnight, the manager of the theater, the assistant manager, two candy girls, and four ushers all were dead, and the newly decorated main lobby of the Le Grande was alive with moving, crawling bodies. . . .

Barry Gillian shifted his position on the seat and tried again to concentrate on the movie. No use. He knew the picture had something to do with devil-worship or possession but he'd lost the plot an hour ago. All he could really concentrate on was Marsha, and the erotic fantasies he hoped would become reality later.

He glanced at her out of the corner of his eye; she was

really something. He had heard a lot of wild stories about her from the other guys at work, about how if she liked you, you really had it made with her. He glanced again at the ample swell of her breats under her thin blouse. He fidgeted in his seat again.

He had had to go to the bathroom for the last twenty minutes now but had figured the picture would end soon. He was sorry now that he had waited, his side was beginning to hurt. He looked down the row of people and decided to wait a little longer; the picture had been on for over two and a half hours now. It *had* to end soon. . . .

He wondered desperately if she liked him or more importantly how much did she like him? He decided to try to find out.

He shifted his position again, putting his arm around her shoulder and drawing her gently to him. She yielded slightly, her movement spreading the opening down the front of her blouse, exposing most of her left breast. He pulled her to him a little more, and succeeded in catching a glimpse of her erect nipple.

Courage. He put his hand on her knee. He left it there for a few seconds, unimpeded, then slowly began moving it up her leg and under her skirt until he reached the top of her thigh. She seemed oblivious of his actions, but her thighs parted slightly, exposing to his touch a small patch of fleecy hair. He felt the soft, warm flesh under his fingertips, and knew he was getting physically excited—except a stabbing pain in his groin made him catch his breath. It was no use trying to wait. If he didn't piss soon he'd die on the spot.

Reluctantly Barry removed his hand, leaned over and whispered to her where he was going. She seemed so engrossed in the movie she didn't even bother looking at him as he got up from his seat and carefully sidled down the row toward the center aisle.

He proceeded up the aisle toward the exit to the lobby, the sticking pain in his side and pressure on his bladder making him walk slowly. As he reached the exit door, he paused for a quick moment to glance at his watch under the dim light—12:10. Good! He estimated that he and Marsha would be back at his apartment and in bed together within an hour. He was smiling as he pushed open the door to the lobby. And screamed, at the same moment trying to jump backward as the mass of spiders swarmed in through the open doorway and poured down the aisle of the crowded theater. He lost his balance and fell clumsily on his back, then began to roll. He screamed once more, then, as the spiders swarmed over him, was mercifully kicked in the head as a panicked man in an aisle seat jumped up and tried to run to safety down the center aisle.

People sitting on the aisle in the back of the theater were the first ones actually to see the spiders pouring through the open doors. They were also the first victims. Most of the others, hearing the screams and commotion coming from the area near the rear exit, could see only shadowy figures beating frantically at themselves, or running from their seats in the darkened theater. People sitting in the balcony up above tried looking over the railing to see what was happening down below. . . .

Jake Coleman thought he heard a scream. He looked up from the girlie magazine he was reading and out of habit glanced at the film projector whirring softly in front of him; everything seemed in order. He unfolded his feet from the stool they rested on, got up from the chair and went over to the observation window in the small projection booth to look down at the audience. He noted that all heads seemed turned toward the right side of the theater. He looked in that direction, saw a flurry of activity by the exit in the rear. People were screaming and running from their seats, tripping and falling in the aisles, colliding with each other to get away from . . . what?

Jake's first thought was that the theater was on fire—except it couldn't be that or he'd have seen flames, smoke. . . . And then he saw them, thousands of them, coming down the aisle, spreading out under the seats. He couldn't make out exactly what they were, but whatever they were, they were big as a man's foot—and, by god, they were attacking and *killing* people. As he watched, disbelieving, the black shapes swarmed over a woman who had fallen in the aisle. She screamed shrilly, beat frantically at them as they clawed and bit her. After a few seconds her body stiffened and she lay still. A man trying to escape into the same aisle tripped over her body . . . no sooner had his hands touched the carpet than he immediately was attacked and covered by the mass of black shapes pouring into the theater.

Horror, panic became contagious, soon spread throughout the theater. People ran from their seats, violently pushed and shoved each other to escape into the aisles—some of them directly into the path of the invading mass. They pushed frantically up the other two aisles toward the exits, but as soon as those doors were pushed open they were met with a new onslaught swarming in on them. They fell screaming, kicking in the aisles, to be trampled by the multitude of feet surging up from behind them.

As Jake watched in dumbfounded shock, the crowd of hysterically stampeding people dwindled noticeably as more and more of them fell before the clawing, biting mass.

Jake turned up the houselights. They were spiders! Huge, black, hairy spiders . . . over six hundred people were being murdered by an army of gigantic spiders!

He heard a clamoring, then screams and shouts from the balcony above him. It was obvious that in their effort to escape people had opened the exit doors and thereby allowed the mass of spiders to invade the balcony. A woman fell screaming, struggling, over the railing, her body almost completely with clinging spiders. She fell with a thud onto the milling crowd below.

A man half fell over the railing but gripped it with his hands and hung suspended in air for a few seconds, not two feet from Jake's window. Spiders clung to every part of his body, clawing and biting at his hands and face. Finally he gave one last agonizing scream of pain and horror, then fell into the crowd below.

Jake watched it all in spite of himself with a kind of disconnected, horrible fascination. This wasn't real, he told himself. It wasn't really happening—couldn't be. The scene he was watching was more like something out of one of the movies he ran. It was like all the times he had run a feature for the first time and had stood by his little observation window and watched, fully engrossed, as earthquakes leveled cities, skyscrapers caught fire and hordes of giant grasshoppers devoured Chicago.

As he watched now, the scene below him seemed to be playing itself out. People weren't running in the aisles any longer, they weren't pushing and shoving or clawing at each other in an attempt to escape. As a matter of fact, he couldn't see the people at all now. All he could see in the theater below him was a living carpet of spiders, crawling over and around, exploring the piles of bodies that filled the aisles and rows. The spiders seemed to be everywhere. They crawled on the seats, they climbed the textured walls of the theater, they were even climbing up the large movie screen, the projected movie making funny rippling images on their backs. Jake finally switched off the movie projector; the show was over.

A faint scratching on the door to the projection room brought him out of his numbed state, like a hard kick in the stomach. They *were* real . . . and now they were trying to get to him. . . .

He quickly went down the short flight of steps, squinted through the peephole in the door. The lobby teemed with them, they covered everything. He swiveled the eyepiece so he could look toward the entrance to the theater; even more were pouring in through the open glass doors—blocking any possible escape. He backed slowly away from the door, afraid even to touch it. He was sure that if he opened that door, even accidentally, he would die just as those unfortunate people in the theater had. . . . The scraping and tapping of claws seemed to be all around him, closing in on him. From where he stood he could see one of the observation windows. As he watched, two spiders tried to cross it, gripping the sides with their claws, then extending their long, hairy legs across the glass. They got halfway across, then dropped off.

There had to be a way . . . the telephone! There was a telephone on the wall in the lobby, right next to the projection room door. If he could reach that phone . . .

There was a smaller door about six inches square mounted in the upper panel of the projection room door that would be just large enough to extend his arm through and, hopefully, to reach the telephone. Slowly and cautiously he unlocked the little door, opened it barely half an inch, ready at the slightest sign of hairy legs to slam it shut again. Through the crack he could see the spiders milling around on the carpet in the lobby, grateful at least that they seemed unable to climb the

197

marbleized walls and that they couldn't climb the enamel-painted projection room door.

He opened the little door all the way, carefully stuck his right arm out through the square hole and reached as far as he could to the left. His fingers touched the side of the telephone. Thank god, I can reach it! He withdrew his arm, dug into his pocket for change. He came up with a quarter, a dime, and two nickels—okay. . . .

Holding the dime between the tips of his thumb and forefinger, he stuck his right arm out through the door again, and strained it as far as he could to the left, the wood frame cutting into his armpit. Now, if he could only get the dime into the coin slot. . . . He moved his fingertips up the side of the phone. He could feel the top now, just a little bit more and—something brushed against his wrist. He jerked his arm back inside, dropping the dime to god-knows-where on the floor. He could hear the clamor of activity outside as the spiders clawed frantically at the bottom of the door, trying to gain a foothold and reach his arm.

Whatever it was that had touched his wrist couldn't have been a spider, he thought, or it would have bitten him. Gingerly, he reached out and over to the same spot again and felt around . . . it was the phone cord. He grabbed the receiver and brought it in through the opening.

Holding the receiver tightly in his left hand, he extended his right arm again, holding one of the nickels in the same way as before. He managed to get the nickel into the coin slot, then repeated the action with the second one. He shifted his position slightly and brought the receiver up to his ear, heard a dial tone. Feeling with his index finger again, he found the dial, then, counting the holes, he located what he was sure was the one for "Operator." He turned the dial.

"Operator. May I help you?" said a metallic female voice in his ear.

"Get me the police, this is an emergency," Jake shouted.

"You may dial that number directly."

"Operator, I can't dial nothin' directly. . . . I'm trapped in a small room in a movie theater surrounded by those goddamn spiders. . . . I only managed to get you by stickin' my arm out through a six-inch hole, now, will you *please* get me the goddamn police? . . ."

A moment of silence. "Well . . . all right, but there's no need to raise your voice. I'm not *deaf,* you know." There followed a series of clicks, then, finally, the phone was ringing.

"Desk. Sergeant Carter—"

"Help me, please, they're going to kill me," Jake was screaming into the phone.

"Name?"

"What the hell does my *name* have to do with it," Jake shouted. "I'm the projectionist at the Le Grande Theater, and the place is overrun with those goddamn spiders—"

"That's not possible, sir, the spider menace is being contained in the evacuated portion of the city. The police department is doing everything within its power to—"

"Don't tell me what the fuck's not possible, I'm lookin' at about a million of the ugly bastards, I just watched them slaughter more than six hundred people, you've got to send someone, do something, or I sure as hell am going to be next!"

A moment of silence. "Are they spread throughout the neighborhood?"

"I don't *know,* but I do know . . . I can see . . . they're knee-deep in this place. Please, you've got to help me, I've got to get out of here."

"Well," the officer said, "it sounds to me like you're in a relatively safe place right where you are. They can't get in, can they?"

"Not as long as I keep the door locked, but—"

"Then I advise you to stay put until morning. In the morning, the spiders will go underground again, the way they've done before."

"But you can't just leave me here," Jake said, panic rising in his voice again. "There's got to be something you can do to get me out of here—"

"There's nothing we can do. There's no effective way of fighting them when they come out in force. Now, just sit tight until morning, then you'll be okay. Relax, try to make the best of it and you'll be safe. I guarantee it."

Jake dropped the receiver onto the floor in the lobby, then closed and locked the little door. He went back up the steps to the projection room and slumped heavily into his chair. The cop was right, he guessed. He'd just have to stick it out till morning. God . . . He took a deep breath, got up and went over to the viewing window of his projection room cubicle and looked down into the interior of the theater.

He pulled his stool over to the viewing window, then sat down with his elbows resting on the sill, and watched with macabre fascination as the milling mass of spiders methodically fed upon their victims.

Chapter 16

MᴄNᴇᴀʟ ᴄʜᴀɴɢᴇᴅ the channel on his television set, then returned to his reclining chair. The recliner seemed to give a groan of pain as he dropped his weight into it; the chair had suffered in this manner for five years now, and the springs sagged badly.

All regularly scheduled television programming had been either delayed or preempted by an endless series of news specials, special reports, bulletins and on-the-spot mobile telecasts, each of which ended with a one-minute piece of recorded conversation that had come to be identified as "The Tape." The Tape was always immediately followed by some radio or television station manager's editorial comments, mostly condemning the officers responsible for what had happened.

Late Saturday night, masses of the spiders had come up in the evacuated areas of Glendale, Eagle Rock and Highland Park, as expected. But swarms of them had also overrun the perimeters and surfaced in the populated sections of Pasadena and Monterey Park. A reporter stationed at the police command post had been on the scene to record the last report from an officer stationed down in the tunnels as spotter. This recording, now frequently played on the air, went:

"Dobbs to Command Post—come in command post—over!" an officer's tension-filled voice echoed over the radio. The officer had to shout in order to be heard over a steadily rising din of scraping and clicking in the background.

"Captain Seiger here," the officer in charge answered. "Go ahead, Dobbs, over!"

"They're coming, captain—moving this way. I can't see them beyond the wall of gas drums yet—but I can hear them moving down the tunnel toward me. I'm going to ignite the drums!"

"Do not—I repeat, do not ignite the drums," Captain Seiger replied. "We need approval from the mayor before we can use them. Do you understand? Over." There were voices in the background as an emergency call was put through to the mayor's office.

"We better do something—and fast!" Dobbs' panicky voice came through. "They're past the drums—coming down the tunnel!"

"Stay at your post, Dobbs," Captain Seiger ordered. "We'll have word in a few moments—"

"Can't! They're almost on top of me, I'm getting

out. . . ." There were scuffling sounds and the echoing clamor seemed to increase audibly, then a long, high-pitched scream.

That final scream on the recording . . . it made McNeal's skin crawl even though he'd heard the tape at least nine times already.

By order of the mayor, preparations were quickly made to evacuate the entire southeastern portion of Los Angeles, right up to the county line. It was an almost impossible task; more than three hundred and fifty thousand people had to be uprooted and moved.

When the authorities came in to search the Pasadena area and count the fatalities, the numbers were staggering: over forty-five hundred people had been slaughtered during the night; over six hundred alone had died in a crowded movie theater invaded by the spiders.

Sunday afternoon had been extremely cloudy and overcast. The masses of spiders had begun surfacing by six o'clock in the late afternoon. By midnight, they had not only infested the already evacuated areas, but had spread out again and were invading populated areas where the round-the-clock evacuation was still taking place—and with disastrous results.

Now, as McNeal sat morbidly watching the latest news bulletin, the latest death toll for the night that had just past was announced. It was the highest yet.

He turned to his wife as she came into the living room carrying his lunch on a tray. "Did you hear the bulletin?" He eyed his lunch unhappily as she set it down on the coffee table in front of him—a dish of cottage cheese, two peach halves, a glass of milk—milk, for god's sake. He was positive that he would never survive his high-protein, low-salt diet.

"Yes, I heard it from the kitchen," she said, shaking her head. "It's horrible."

"Horrible isn't the word for it, and there's no damn way to stop them. . . ."

"George, do you think there's any chance of them spreading in this direction?"

"The way things are going . . ."

The telephone rang, and it was Bryson telling him his R and R was over, sorry about that, and that they were both—as the only surviving eyewitnesses to what was going on in the tunnels—expected to attend another meeting that afternoon at City Hall.

McNeal was relieved, at least to be back in action, even if he had to put up with those eggheads and their yakking.

DR. BENJAMIN got off the elevator on the sixth floor of the science building, walked down the hall. He felt physically exhausted from spending almost three hours stuck in the extraordinary crunch of traffic. Between the never-ending stream of cars and trucks trying desperately to escape the city and the long convoys of military vehicles traveling in every direction it was damn near impossible to navigate.

He couldn't avoid thinking back over the last forty-eight hours of terror he had just gone through, his mind still holding onto traces of some lingering dread. The hours, dragging by, minute by agonizing minute as he lay in his hospital bed; the horror of possibly being infested with spider eggs, then the doctor coming in, smiling, and telling him that all the tests had proved negative. . . . Most of the bandages had been removed from his left hand and arm; he now wore a plastic shield lightly bandaged to his wrist. He had been assured by the doctor that the arm and wrist would heal in a short period of time. . . .

He was surprised to find the door to his office unlocked, even more surprised—and pleased, too—as he entered his office. "Christine . . . what are you doing here? . . . how did you get in? . . ."

She dropped the papers she was reading and came quickly around the desk to him. "The door was unlocked when I got here, I wanted to go over our notes again. . . ." She looked at him intensely. "Harold . . . I was very worried about you," and she put her arms around him and drew him close to her. "How do you feel?"

"Better," he answered, "especially now. . . . Thank you for being there, Christine. . . ."

They stood in each other's arms a few moments more, saying nothing, each comforted by the warmth of the other.

"Have you been to the lab yet?" he finally asked.

"No, it was locked, I didn't have a key. Anyhow, I knew you were coming here and I thought it best to wait for you."

He unlocked the doors to the main lab, and upon entering was surprised that nothing had been touched, nothing straightened or tidied. Everything, in fact, was exactly as it had been almost three days earlier when he had been attacked . . . books and equipment still lay scattered and broken on the floor, spilled liquids and chemicals stained the floor, walls and tables, broken glass crunched underfoot as they walked to the back of the lab to put on their lab coats.

"I'm afraid I'm responsible for this mess," she said. "After they took you to the hospital I left orders that nothing be disturbed or touched in here."

He nodded. "We'll salvage whatever equipment we can from this mess and improvise as best we can."

As she began picking up books and equipment and piling usable items on a lab table, he went over to the table containing the vivariums, looked at the smashed tank with disgust. How in the world could it have been broken like that? It looked as if it had been smashed from the outside. He looked around for something that might have fallen over and hit it, saw nothing. He lightly tapped on the glass side of one of the other tanks with his knuckle, immediately drawing his hand back from the expected attack.

The spiders in the vivarium did not move.

He watched the spiders closely, knocked on the glass again, this time harder.

The spiders still did not move.

He picked up a book and rapped the side of the tank as hard as he could with it, moving the entire tank at least two inches on the surface of the table.

Three of the spiders flopped over on their backs from the concussion, then lay still with the others.

The spiders were all dead.

He could not believe his eyes. Dead! Every last one of them was dead! How? Why? *What* had killed them? They had to find out, and quickly. . . .

"Christine, come over here. . . ."

She rushed over to him. "Harold, what is it? Are you feeling sick—"

"No, no, I'm fine—but, *look* . . ." and he pointed to the vivarium containing the dead spiders. "Look at them, Christine, they're all *dead.* . . ."

She stared at the dead creatures for a few moments, then glanced at the other tank, which also contained dead spiders. "Could they have starved to death?" she suggested, seeing the empty water dishes. "Nobody's been in here to feed them for at least three days—"

"No, they couldn't have starved. Look at them. They show absolutely no signs of dehydration. By their stiffened appearance I'd say they've been dead for at least thirty-six hours." He looked at her. "Christine . . . it was something else, something we've done or used . . . something right here in this laboratory that's proved fatal to them. We've got to find out what. . . ."

"We'll need help," she sensibly pointed out. "It would take much too long for us to finish all the research and tests necessary to pinpoint the cause. We've got to contact those two men from the Smithsonian, enlist their aid." She took his hand and they started back to his office to make the call. "They're in a meeting right now with the mayor and governor—I was invited but after I heard the solution they're suggesting I wanted no part of it."

She glanced at the desk clock in his office. "It's already three-twenty," she said, picking up the telephone. "I hope to god we can still reach them."

THE GOVERNOR of California had flown in that morning to attend the meeting accompanied by two structural geologists from the California Institute of Technology and a representative from the Atomic Energy Commission.

"I sure don't like the looks of this," McNeal commented to Bryson. "When they start bringing in people like those geologists and the Atomic Energy Commission. . . ."

"If it means what I think it means," Bryson said under his voice, "this city can kiss its ass goodbye."

McNeal and Bryson had a short conference with the scientists from the Smithsonian, and after a brief discussion outlining the facts everyone took seats around the conference table.

Mayor Bradshaw got to his feet. "Gentlemen, Governor Harris, we must come up with a solution, no matter how drastic, to rid the city of this awful menace. At a meeting earlier this morning, Professors Winkler and

Meyers suggested what may be the only possible answer. We're here, now, to discuss its feasibility."

"Perhaps some explanation of our predicament is in order," Professor Winkler suggested. "After examining copies of Dr. Benjamin's and Dr. Selby's notes we carried their tests and experiments one or two steps further. We examined, then dissected, most of the two hundred specimens caught in the evacuated area Saturday and found them to be almost totally hermaphroditic—most of them carrying fertilized eggs. Some of the specimens could not have been more than two or three months old, and although much smaller than the others their reproductive organs were completely mature. There's no doubt that these young spiders can and will bear living offspring at their next egg cycle."

McNeal and Bryson were then asked to tell what they'd observed down in the tunnels, and they gave details about what they'd earlier described as "the nursery" and told how the entire tunnel they had traveled through was scattered with egg sacs, "tens of thousands of egg sacs covering the walls and ceiling for as far as you could see. . . ."

"That's the very point we're discussing," Professor Winkler said. "A rough estimate of the spider population at this point would be somewhere around fifteen million, maybe more. The population has grown so that large groups of them are moving away, spreading out in the tunnel system to begin new colonies in the same fashion that ants and bees break away from the parent unit to start new hives and colonies—just the way Dr. Selby predicted they would. This breaking up and spreading out of the colony would explain how they could infest the evacuated areas of Glendale, Eagle Rock and Highland Park and also be far enough south to invade Pasadena at the same time." He paused to refer to some notes from his briefcase. "Gentlemen, this mutant species has all the instincts, all the bloodthirsty qualities of a huge school of piranha. Their driving instinct, literally, is to attack and kill anything that crosses their path. Next to this drive, all other instincts—even the instinct to survive—come in second. These creatures are, without a doubt, the deadliest we've ever faced—"

"Isn't there any poison or insecticide that would be effective?" the mayor said.

"Their population is growing at such a fantastic rate we've nothing that could effectively stop or even curb it. Statistically, every ten seconds at least fifty spiders lay approximately eight hundred to a thousand eggs, maybe more. The colony consists almost totally of females, and each one, theoretically, can reproduce itself by almost a thousand. We can estimate that within two weeks the whole storm-drain system—all eight hundred square miles of it—will be completely infested with them." He paused and looked at the stunned faces. "At that point they will begin spreading out to other areas—the San Gabriel Valley, the San Fernando Valley, Long Beach, Santa Ana, and begin *new* colonies that will grow and redouble themselves and spread up and down the California coast. They'll infest other cities, other areas, until they've covered the whole state. . . ." He paused to let his words sink in. "If we don't take the necessary steps to stop it immediately this horror will spread across the whole country."

There were a few moments of silence as the men exchanged shocked, disbelieving looks. Finally the governor spoke. "I've been in touch with the President, he has empowered me to use whatever methods or weapons are necessary—"

"But you said before that there was no way to stop or even control these damn things," the mayor said.

"They can definitely be stopped," Professor Winkler said. "But they must be stopped completely, totally. They must be annihilated. If so much as one or two of them were to survive then this whole thing could probably begin all over again." He took a deep breath. "I am speaking of using some type of nuclear device—"

"You must be crazy," the mayor shouted, getting to his feet. "You want to drop a hydrogen bomb—on Los Angeles, for god's sake? . . ."

"I was not referring to a hydrogen bomb in the sense that you think of one. I was suggesting the possible use of a neutron bomb."

"As I understand it," Governor Harris put in, "a neutron bomb only affects organic life. The city, itself, will remain intact."

"But what about polluting the atmosphere and the buildings with radioactivity . . . with fallout?" the mayor asked, shaking his head. "I find very little consolation in the idea of having the city of Los Angeles left perfectly preserved as a radioactive deathtrap for the next hundred years."

"The city's lost already," Governor Harris said with finality. "The way they're multiplying and spreading, the city of Los Angeles and its surrounding areas will have to be completely evacuated anyhow in order to protect the people from certain death. At that point the city of Los Angeles will be a ghost town. . . . If this menace is not completely annihilated this city, and eventually the entire state, will never be habitable again."

For the first time Henry Jessup, from the Atomic Energy Commission, spoke. "I'm afraid you people have been misinformed about the use and effectiveness of a neutron bomb. A neutron bomb is primarily an air-burst device, and would not be totally effective as long as these creatures are entrenched in the tunnels beneath the city.

The very nature of those concrete tunnels would serve to shield most of the creatures from the radiation. No," he said, as if debating the point with himself, "a neutron bomb would definitely not do it. . . . I would suggest the use of a thermonuclear device for maximum effectiveness." He looked around the table at the astonished, shocked faces. "Gentlemen," he said as though lecturing a class, "we've come a long way in our technology since Hiroshima and Nagasaki. We've now developed a 'clean bomb' in which radioactivity is no longer a problem." He actually smiled. "Fallout is inconsequential from these new bombs, and radioactivity is kept at a bare two percent. On the other hand, the thermal radiation—the fireball—is of an extremely high heat intensity . . . and the blast-shock these devices produce would be perfect for the subterranean tunnels we're dealing with here."

"If we do agree to use this device, will one of these bombs be sufficient to cover the entire area?" Governor Harris asked, giving Jessup a peculiar look, as if he suspected he was dealing with a madman, and was shocked to hear himself speaking almost blandly about the use of nuclear weapons on a city.

"No. One device would not be enough," Jessup said. He opened his briefcase and took a large detailed map of the city which he spread out on the table in front of him. "I would suggest the use of three devices, placed here, here, and here," and he pointed out the locations on the map with his finger. "Placed in these strategic locations they would have maximum effectiveness, especially where the thermal radiation limits and blast-force intersect. In short, three bombs will have no trouble completely vaporizing the city and everything in it." He sat back, his smooth face untroubled, calm.

"This guy can't be for real," McNeal whispered to Bryson.

Bryson nodded his agreement.

The mayor just sat shaking his head. "I can't believe this," he muttered to himself.

"As I understand it, there could be side effects from these devices," the governor put in, looking toward the two geologists. "Exactly *what* side effects?"

"There could definitely be side effects, probably severe ones at that," said Alan Tate, the older of the two geologists. "As you all probably know, California is cursed with a structural phenomenon known as the San Andreas fault." From his attaché case he produced geological maps and prints of the western coast of the United States. "This geological fault," he said, tracing his finger along a dark blue line running up the California coast, "runs clear from Baja Mexico through the coastal part of this state, then connecting with two other fault concentrations, runs up through Oregon, Washington, and into Canada." He selected another chart. "These faults, or rather series of faults, are deep fissures in the earth's crust held together by stresses in the formation of the rock comprising the continental shelf. This series of faults, especially the San Andreas, is constantly under terrific pressures in both horizontal and vertical directions." He looked up from his charts. "I'll skip the idiosyncrasies of the San Andreas fault, or the technical reasons for them. It's enough to say that we have an extremely delicate balance at work here, and to trigger an explosion—or series of explosions—of the magnitude you gentlemen are suggesting might very possibly rupture the fault at this location here." He indicated a place along the heavy blue line with his finger. "You could possibly start a chain reaction that would run the length of the fault series, relieving and changing pressures and stresses." He looked directly at the governor. "The outcome of such a chain reaction could possibly be the rupturing of the entire San Andreas and San Jacinto fault systems, and if this occurred the western continental shelf—about seven hundred miles of it—would break off and crumble and slip into the Pacific Ocean. . . ."

In the silence that followed Tate neatly folded his maps and charts, put them back into his briefcase. "If this occurred," he added, "then geographically speaking the western seacoast would be located somewhere around Bakersfield, which is now in the middle of the Mojave Desert."

The telephone by the door was ringing. Bryson, who was closest to the door, got up to answer it. "Professor," he said, motioning to Professor Meyers, "it's Dr. Selby and it sounds important." He handed the phone to Meyers.

"You sure as hell paint a black picture," the governor was saying. "We're damned if we do, and we're certainly damned if we don't." He leaned back in his chair, leaned forward again, his mind apparently made up. "We'll begin evacuating the entire state as soon as humanly possible. I'll notify the President again, fill him in. . . ." He made a helpless gesture. "It seems we'll have to sacrifice the city, the entire state, if necessary. What other choice do we have?"

"None," Professor Winkler said, nodding in agreement. "It must be done."

"Winkler!" Professor Meyers broke in, excitement in his voice. "We're needed at the main laboratory at the university immediately. . . ." He turned to the governor. "They've discovered the test specimens dead—the cause of their death unknown."

"Meaning? . . ."

"Meaning that *something* has proved lethal to them. We need the time to discover what." He looked at the governor. "You *must* hold off with this . . . give us time to do tests . . . this may be the break we've needed—"

"But can we afford to wait? . . ."

"You *must*—we must have time to at least try to find the cause of their death . . . this nuclear device must be held as an absolute last resort."

The governor looked like a man being torn apart inside, then his expression firmed. "I pray we're making the right choice," he said, spreading his hands. "All right . . . we'll wait."

Chapter 17

WHEN MEYERS and Winkler arrived at the main lab in the science building they found Dr. Benjamin and Dr. Selby at work separating usable instruments and equipment from the wreckage around them.

"I'm glad you could come so quickly," Dr. Benjamin said, shaking their hands enthusiastically. "We've only a few more items to put in order, then we'll be ready to begin."

Dr. Selby nodded hello to them, then went back to sorting through the debris.

"You realize, of course, that this could be just a fluke

of some kind," Professor Meyers said. "It doesn't necessarily mean—"

"Of course, it does, you examined those specimens, you know as well as I do that you couldn't kill them any way short of running them over with a truck. They had to come in contact with something—something lethal to them, right here in this laboratory. All we have to do is discover what." He picked up one of the hairy corpses. "I'm hoping that an autopsy on these dead specimens will tell us the what."

Although they didn't share Benjamin's high pitch of enthusiasm they couldn't argue with his logic, and set to work, each dissecting and studying a different specimen. . . .

Two hours later they had isolated the cause of death: each specimen had an infected inflammation in its book lungs; the lung tissue, after filling with mucus and fluid, had turned brittle and inflexible; the spiders had, literally, suffocated to death.

They were close! A few more tests . . . a few more experiments. . . . They immediately began another series of tests, analyzing blood and tissue samples under microscope. Surely they'd find the answer here. . . . But after several minutes Dr. Benjamin, looking up from his microscope, rubbed his eyes and said, "Nothing." He turned to Christine, who was seated next to him doing workups on one of the samples. "These blood and tissue samples show a complete lack of protein matter, but I can't find any cause for it . . . there are no visible organisms, not a trace of chemical matter. . . ." He shrugged in confusion. "Yet this tissue is completely stripped of protein. How?"

"Perhaps some sort of bacteria?"

"That wouldn't be likely," he said. "To my knowledge there isn't a single type of bacteria that feeds on protein to this degree. Anyhow," he added, tapping the side of the microscope, "at two thousand power, bacteria would show up in this about the size of small rocks. No, it's got to be something else, something smaller. . . ."

Their eyes met, as a single thought seemed to occur to them simultaneously. "Meyers . . . Winkler," Dr. Benjamin called. "What's your knowledge of viruses?"

"Little or nothing," Professor Meyers admitted, stopping what he was doing and coming over to where Benjamin and Selby sat. "Virology is a little out of our field."

Dr. Benjamin nodded. "Then we must get people in here who know . . . a virus just may be our culprit . . . or rather our salvation."

Professor Meyers telephoned Dr. Perelli and briefed him on the discoveries they'd made and what they suspected. Perelli agreed to send over a team of virologists on staff at the health department to study the samples and isolate and classify any virus growth present.

Professor Meyers went back to the lab. "Dr. Perelli agrees to—Dr. Benjamin, are you all right?"

He had staggered against one of the lab tables as a wave of dizziness came over him. "I'll be fine, just a little dizzy. . . ."

"Well . . . Dr. Perelli is sending a team of virologists," Professor Meyers said, still watching Benjamin closely. He touched the doctor's arm. "Are you sure you're all right? You look a little pale."

"I'm all right now," Dr. Benjamin assured him. "The dizziness has passed. . . ."

The main lab was still in a state of shambles, the facilities limited, so they gathered all the salvageable equipment and moved it over to the biology lab, where there was also specialized equipment that would be of particular use in their new research. . . .

AFTER FOUR hours of silent, intense work since arriving, the virologist named Peter Howell spoke, his voice startling everyone. "We can, I think, now say that these specimens' deaths were caused by a virus, or rather a combination of two or more viruses—some type of mutant strain."

Benjamin thought briefly of the samples of microbiological cultures they had selected, then left out over night. The crushed, smashed remnants of them were still scattered throughout the main laboratory. Two or more of those cultures had obviously reproduced and mutated together, forming a mutant strain of virus that was fatal to the mutant spiders. It was fantastic! He had to laugh out loud at the wonderful irony of it. . . .

"The important question," Professor Meyers said, an urgency in his voice, "is, can this—this mutant strain of virus—be used as a lethal antidote against the spiders?"

Howell shrugged. "Well, we definitely know the cause of death, but with the infinite variety of mutant strains possible when a number of cultures are breeding and crossbreeding together, it's impossible to know exactly which one would be effective. Narrowing it down to discover exactly which strain was lethal would be nothing more than a process of elimination —but it will take time—"

"And time," Winkler said, "is something we've damn little of."

"I realize that," Howell said, "but, also, after we isolate the right one, we still have to determine the effect of it on other living things."

On a hunch, and a dismal one at that, Dr. Benjamin went into the alcove off the main lab, where the laboratory animals were kept. If the same strain of virus that had been fatal to the spiders also proved fatal to mammals, it would, he thought, have to be destroyed. A mutant strain like that would then represent an infectious plague that could threaten everything . . . everybody. . . .

The laboratory animals were all dead.

Autopsies on four guinea pigs and two large white rats showed they had all died from massive deterioration of their *nervous* system. Thank god . . . they'd been killed by an entirely different strain of virus. There was still hope. . . . Dr. Benjamin leaned against one of the lab tables as another wave of dizziness hit him. He hadn't realized until that moment what a terrific strain the last few hours had been on him. His left arm and wrist were throbbing painfully, he had a curiously nauseating sensation in the pit of his stomach and his chest felt tight.

"Christine," he said, calling her over to him. "We've done all we can at the moment . . . and, well . . . I'm afraid I'm not feeling so well. . . . I think I'd better get a little rest before I collapse on you completely. . . ."

"I think so too," she agreed, looking at him with concern. "Do you want some help—?"

"No, no, I can make it fine . . . you ought to get some rest too. You must be at least as tired as I am."

"I'll just sit over there with my feet up for a while," she said. "That's really all I'll need." She gave him a quick kiss on the cheek. "Now go rest," she said, smiling at him. "You really do look beat."

Using the wall for support and calling on all his will power to keep from stumbling, he carefully made his way out the door and slowly down the hall. As he entered his office, the telephone on his desk began ringing. He sat down heavily in the chair behind his desk and shook his head to clear the dizziness. The telephone continued its urgent ringing, the noise cutting through his head like a knife. He sat, blankly staring at it for another few seconds, his head swimming with dizziness. Finally he closed his eyes and shook his head once again, then picked up the receiver. "Yes?"

"Dr. Benjamin? Thank god I finally reached you. Is it true what Perelli tells me? You've found some way to beat this thing?" Governor Harris' voice exploded excitedly, blaring in Benjamin's ear and almost causing him to drop the receiver.

"We haven't exactly found it yet," he answered slowly, finding it extremely difficult to concentrate on what he was saying. "Yes, the specimens were all dead, and we know it was definitely caused by a mutant strain of virus. When it's isolated it should be effective . . . but we haven't yet succeeded in isolating the right strain. . . . As you undoubtedly know, we have experts working on that. . . ."

"I don't understand. You said the virus caused the spiders' death."

"That's true . . . but with the breeding and crossbreeding of these virus cultures thousands of new strains and cross-strains are possible . . . we must find the right one—"

"There's a time-element here . . . if you don't find it damn soon we may have to continue with . . . other alternatives."

"It's just a matter of isolating the correct one, we'll do it," Benjamin said, sounding more hopeful than he felt. "The virus we're looking for attacks the spiders' book lungs. . . ." It was a major effort but he felt he needed to explain to the governor, who sounded as if he might otherwise do something rash. "This type of lung is unique in nature—only spiders have them. We also found all the laboratory test animals dead in the room next to the laboratory. The virus that killed those animals couldn't have killed the spiders, and the same is true in reverse. . . . I mean, for example, the virus that causes hoof-and-mouth disease in cattle would have no effect on dogs and cats. . . ."

"You've no idea how long it might take to isolate the virus we need?"

"It could be within the next hour, or it could take . . . much longer. We have to be very careful with these mutated cultures. The biological cultures I originally selected would not have been harmful to people, but when you're dealing with cross-mutations, anything is possible. . . . Excuse me, I'm afraid I'm feeling rather tired, I guess it's the strain of work, the hospital, contact with the viruses in the main laboratory. . . . I promise you, governor, either Dr. Selby or I will contact you as soon as we have something positive to tell you. Now, if you'll excuse me—" He hung up.

He shook his head again. The dizziness had subsided somewhat and his vision had cleared, but he still had the queasy feeling in his stomach and his neck and shoulders were tight and sore with tension. He laid his head across his arms on the top of the desk and closed his eyes. Within moments he had fallen asleep.

"DR. BENJAMIN? Are you in there?" Someone was knocking loudly on his office door, calling out his name urgently.

He opened his eyes and sat up, trying to reorient himself, to shake the fuzziness from his brain. His office was dark . . . how long had he been asleep? It seemed as though he'd only nodded off for a moment. . . . He stretched his arms above his head and took a deep breath, then coughed wetly. The uncomfortable tightness in his chest had worsened, and when he breathed he wheezed slightly. He coughed again. A bronchial cough? That's just what he needed now—a damn chest cold. . . . He stood up and carefully felt his way around the side of the desk. "Yes . . . what is it?" he called, then coughed

221

again—that cough really hurt his chest.

"Dr. Benjamin, we've been looking all over for you!" There was relief and excitement in the voice. "We've isolated the virus, we've got it . . . are you there, did you hear me? . . ."

Moving carefully across the dark office, he flipped on the overhead lights and unlocked the door. He took a quick glance at his watch. Good lord, he thought, I've been out for more than fourteen hours. . . .

He opened the door and they all came filing in, the virologist Peter Howell in the lead, Christine and the others pushing in closely behind. All of them wore broad, excited grins. Howell held up a glass vial containing a thick-looking amber liquid randomly streaked with a greenish substance.

"This virus—or should I say super-virus—is deoxyribonucleic-acid based. It feeds and reproduces exclusively on organic protein. In order to produce and nurture it, all that's needed is a protein solution. It thrives on it!"

Benjamin nodded, smiled weakly. "I'm afraid I'm fairly stupid about virology"—he coughed again— "could you explain? . . ."

"Sure, if you'll bear with some basics," Howell said, putting down the vial and sitting on the edge of the desk. "A virus, as you know, is considered the smallest of all living organisms. It consists of a protein shell surrounding a core of nucleic acid. It enters the living cells of animals and plants, feeding and reproducing itself within those cells and assimilating the cell's protein content. By doing this, it destroys the cell and must enter another one in order to survive and reproduce again." He held up the vial again. "This virus is definitely an animal-attacking virus. It mutated with two other strains—exactly which ones we haven't discovered yet—and formed what, if you'll forgive the dramatics, I call a super-virus. It's definitely superior in content and construction to most. It will attack and destroy other strains of virus, and also many kinds of bacteria. After this strain is thoroughly tested it may even prove effective against such diseases as smallpox, rabies, maybe even the common cold. There's no telling what it can do—"

"All well and good," Benjamin said, "but let's stick to the problem at hand. Exactly how effective will this virus be against the spiders?"

"Dr. Benjamin, it has *already* proved to be lethal, a hundred percent effective!" Professor Meyers put in. "Perhaps I should explain, it's more in my field. . . . In most air-breathing animal life this virus would attack the respiratory system because the lungs, bronchial canals and such are constructed of particularly soft and yielding tissue. In the higher forms of life, mammals, amphibians and the like, the body produces natural defenses to disease by the way of antibodies in the bloodstream. These antibodies, as you know, will combat and destroy the invading virus—even a mutant strain of this kind. The only effect this virus might have on a man, for example, would be the traces of a mild attack of pneumonia. With the use of antibiotics such as streptomycin or penicillin the effect of the virus should be no worse than a very bad chest cold—"

"But the lower, more primitive forms of life *don't* produce such antibodies," Dr. Benjamin broke in, now understanding fully and beginning to share the others' enthusiasm, "and would have no defense for the invading virus. . . . The spiders would have no defense whatsoever—"

"Exactly," Professor Meyers said, smiling. "They're

223

defenseless to the point that once the virus invades their book lungs it destroys the tissue so that it's left brittle and unyielding. The lung tissue, literally, begins to crack and flake—destruction is total. Of the over two hundred living specimens we've already tested this virus on, in every case side effects appeared within ninety minutes and death resulted within six hours. When introduced to them in an airborne state, the specimens breathed the virus directly into their lungs, and without exception were dead within the same six hours. When we introduced it through food or water, the side effects took longer to become apparent but the result was the same."

"So in order to use this virus," Christine said, "we need to be very careful not to start an airborne epidemic that could completely wipe out the entire insect and spider populations throughout the world. That would be quite possible, and a disaster in its own right."

"Yes. . . . Well," Meyers went on, "once introduced, this virus seems to run rampant, spreading and reproducing at a astounding rate and destroying the tissue completely. But, after the tissue has been destroyed and it has nowhere else to spread to, the virus tends to die right along with the host. It doesn't seem to have the ability to detach itself from its host and travel any long distances. It will, though, travel from one spider to another in closed quarters. And *that* is all we'll need."

"From what you've told me and Christine has just properly pointed out, I'd certainly suggest not using this virus in any airborne fashion," Dr. Benjamin said. "It would be safer and much more controlled if we were to, say, introduce it into the spiders' food supply—" He stopped abruptly, seized with a fit of racking coughs that made his chest feel as though it were on fire. After a moment the coughing ceased; he painfully cleared his throat, wiped the perspiration from his face and neck, then dabbed at his tearing eyes with his handkerchief.

After asking if he was all right and being assured that he was, Meyers said, "I'm not too clear what exactly you mean when you suggest introducing the virus into their food supply?"

". . . the use of animals of some kind," Benjamin said. "Inoculate these animals with massive doses of the virus, then send them into the tunnels. Considering the spiders' ferocity, the rest should take care of itself. Because of their size and bulk, I'd suggest using . . . well, cows, for example. They'd be fed on by the spider mass, thereby spreading the virus—" His words ended in another fit of hacking coughs. "You were right," he said after a moment, noticing the look on Meyers' face, "I was exposed to the virus contaminating the main laboratory longer than you, and that along with my weakened condition after my injuries seems to have made me the first one to contract—a chest cold."

Christine quickly phoned the medical center, which was housed in the huge conglomeration of buildings on the UCLA campus. She spoke to one of the resident doctors, explained how they had all been exposed to a flu-causing virus. The doctor agreed to visit them and administer strong antibiotics. She then called the microbiology wing of the medical center and arranged to have the entire laboratory wing of the science building decontaminated.

"Can you produce more of this virus if necessary?" Dr. Benjamin asked Howell.

"There's enough virus culture in that vial to wipe out every insect and spider on earth," Howell told him. "I doubt you'd need more than that."

"Uh . . . of course, I'm sure you're right," Dr. Benjamin said, feeling uncomfortable about his lack of knowledge in the field. "Well, I'll contact the governor and mayor and get as much arranged as I can before tomorrow morning." He looked at his watch. "It's almost three A.M. now, but under the circumstances I would doubt if we'll find anyone sleeping." He picked up the phone and began dialing. "We've done our job, which is what counts right now. I advise us all to get at least a few hours rest before we meet at the riverbed and, hopefully, finally put an end to this business." He looked at each of them. "I don't know how to thank you all for the brilliant work you've done. I'm sure it won't be forgotten."

The scientists left the office, still talking and congratulating each other. Christine stayed. Taking a seat in front of the desk, she waited patiently while he made his call to the governor and told him the good news.

"That's wonderful . . . can it be used immediately?"

"Not until sunrise. It's necessary for the spider mass to be closely confined within the tunnels."

"Any chance this new strain of virus could be harmful to people?"

Dr. Benjamin explained about the possible symptoms of an acute bronchial infection that could be treated in the same way as pneumonia, and advised the governor to tell the health department to gear up for an outbreak of bronchial pneumonia, to stock up on antibiotics. He filled him in on the doctor from the medical center coming to inoculate the scientists. He assured him that they intended to keep the use of the virus as contained as possible, and so they'd need some cattle, about fifty head, to be trucked out to the entrance to the storm-drain tunnels as early as possible in the morning—

"Cattle?" the governor asked, understandably surprised by the request.

"That's right. They'll make ideal host animals to

spread the virus among the spider masses. I hope you can arrange for it at this short notice—"

"They'll be there. Will you need anything more?"

"No . . . except—could you do me a personal favor?"

"Name it."

"Contact Lieutenant McNeal and brief him on what's about to happen and where. Please tell him that I personally invite him to attend. He's been involved in this . . . matter right from its beginning. I'm quite sure he'll want to be there when it ends."

"I'll be glad to take care of that," the governor assured him.

"I can't guarantee we'll be completely successful," Dr. Benjamin said. "Only time will tell that . . . but at least we have our weapon. . . . Goodbye, Governor."

He cradled the telephone, then turned and looked at Christine through tired, red eyes. "And how are *you* feeling?" he asked, his voice rough and scratchy. "Has the virus affected you yet?"

"No, not yet. Oh, I suppose it will, but at the moment I feel pretty damn good." She looked at him and smiled. "But you, look at you. You really look like hell."

"Feel like it too," he said, then turned serious. "Christine . . . when this is finally over . . . well, what are your plans, what do you intend to do? . . ."

She came around the desk and stood for a moment, looking intently at him. "You mean about us?"

"Yes"—watching her closely—"I mean about us. . . . Look, I realize we've only known each other a few days and I've no illusions about my attractiveness to a woman like you . . . but I just wanted you to know that in these last few days you've brought a warmth, a specialness into my life that I'd hate to lose, if there's a chance you feel anything of the same. . . . Anyway, I sure as hell don't want to lose you to that damned desert project again." He forced himself to smile.

She looked at him seriously. "Harold, I feel a good deal the same, but there'll be time later to talk about it . . . plenty of time. Just be patient . . . please?"

Chapter 18

MCNEAL, ALONG with Bryson, arrived at the riverbed entrance to the drainage system shortly before dawn. The entire area along the riverbed, stretching for almost a mile, was brightly lit by hundreds of huge floodlights mounted on high metal tripods. Many of the floodlights were pointed directly into the entrance to the tunnels to make it easier to detect anything emerging from the tunnels. Beyond the point where the light ended at the entrance the tunnels were engulfed in inky blackness.

McNeal had to admit he'd felt flattered to receive a personal call from the governor telling him about the discovery of the virus, explaining how it was to be used and asking him to be there. He parked his car now near a portable corral constructed from sections of chain-link fencing that was to contain the cattle when they arrived. At one end of the corral was a fenced pathway just wide enough for the cows to pass through it single file, when they would each get an injection containing a massive dose of the virus. At the end of the fenced pathway stood three large vans so crowded with laboratory and medical equipment that they almost overflowed at the open side and back doors.

"George, what do you think will happen if this virus business doesn't work?" Bryson asked as they got out of the car.

"Well, I have a friend on the police force in New York. I suggest we all move there," McNeal said dismally. "I don't have to tell you what this city, or the state for that matter, will look like after crazy sons of bitches like that Jessup character blow the hell out of it." He spotted Benjamin, Selby and the other professors a short distance away, and in a loud argument. He couldn't make out their words but it was clear that they were disagreeing with Dr. Benjamin. Finally Benjamin turned and walked away, Dr. Selby tugging at his arm, asking him to listen to reason. McNeal quickly turned his back and tried to avoid them. Too late, they'd seen him and were motioning for him and Bryson to join them. Given no choice, they walked over.

". . . he has got to understand that we are a great deal more useful supervising and directing this operation," Professor Meyers was saying as McNeal and Bryson arrived. "And if by any chance this virus should happen to fail, then we would have to be able to continue research. We would be the only hope the city would have." He looked at the others, who wholeheartedly agreed with him. "Then we'll continue with the original volunteer plan. After introducing the virus into the cows' bloodstreams we should allow about an hour for it to spread throughout their circulatory systems. At that point we'll give them the booster protein shot." Again, everyone agreed. "Then two cows should be herded into each of the connecting tunnels. We'll need men to continue prodding them deeper into the tunnels, until they've contacted the spider masses." He turned to McNeal. "Lieutenant, will you see to it that we have enough . . . volunteers?"

"They'll have to be volunteers," McNeal said firmly. "I won't order my men to go down into those tunnels." He glanced at Bryson, who nodded.

After the tentative plans had been made, McNeal left the group, hoping to find someone with coffee. . . . "Lieutenant, Lieutenant McNeal . . ." Benjamin was calling, waving at him. McNeal turned reluctantly and walked over to where Benjamin and Selby were standing.

"Lieutenant, you've got the authority—you've got to help me convince them. Those fools are so wrapped up in their own importance they can't see the truth. We're the ones who should drive those cattle into the tunnels, not some well-meaning terrified laymen. We should do it because only a trained eye would see and understand what it's observing. The policeman you pick would, understandably, be thinking of nothing more than how quickly he could drive the cows into the tunnel, then get himself out of there again. If I were to go I'd notice any apparent differences in their behavior pattern, any characteristic deviation. If the virus were to fail I could return with valuable, perhaps vital information for their eventual destruction—"

"But you can't take that kind of chance, throwing your life away. . . ." Christine was protesting.

231

"Is my life any more or less important than the men the lieutenant here will send? If anything, it would make more sense for me to take the chance to gain some vital information than for them to risk their lives just to run an errand. . . . Lieutenant McNeal, you're the one picking the so-called volunteers. Well, damn it, pick me—"

"No," Christine broke in. "Lieutenant, he's sick with bronchial pneumonia, he's been injured, he's completely worn out physically—"

"Christine, it doesn't take physical strength to see and observe." He turned back to McNeal. "Lieutenant, I'm not trying to be a hero. It's really not a question of preferences. It's just something that makes sense and—"

"I'm sorry, I can't do it," McNeal said finally. "As Dr. Selby here pointed out, you're not a well man and definitely in no condition for what you're suggesting." He patted him on the shoulder. "And, anyhow," he added, almost as an afterthought, "I personally don't have the authority—"

"It's not authority I need, it's common sense. I am the *logical* choice to go." He turned in disgust and walked off.

She started after him until McNeal, gently taking her arm, said, "Give him time to think. This seems to be very important to him."

She reluctantly agreed, and then a loud air-horn blasted and a caravan of immense cattle trucks was seen moving slowly down the access road and across the dry riverbed. The air was filled with bellows and mooing, and the unmistakable odor of the cows. The lead truck pulled as close as it could to the gate of the corral. When it was in position, two men got out of the cab, swung the large side doors open and proceeded to unload the cows. The other trucks followed suit.

As the cows, herded and prodded along, came one at a time through the chute, Professors Meyers and Winkler

232

injected each one in the rump with a prepared hypodermic needle, after which they were prodded the rest of the way down the narrow path and into the corral.

Within an hour and a half the cattle began showing definite symptoms of the virus invading their system . . . they became restless and nervous, were subject to minor skin spasms along their back and flanks and began showing a distinct difficulty in breathing. An injection of protein solution was then administered directly into the bloodstream to help strengthen the virus even more. They would soon be ready.

McNeal, somewhat to his surprise, had no trouble in getting the needed volunteers. Almost all seemed willing to help make the operation a success—they'd seen the consequences of failure at firsthand. McNeal was damned proud of them. He selected thirty men and told them to go over to the medical van to be briefed by Professors Meyers and Winkler, then went over to where he had noticed a group of officers congregating around the rear of a large supply truck. He found Bryson standing with the others having coffee and doughnuts.

"You could have told me," McNeal growled, pouring himself a cup of coffee.

"Sorry. . . . George, how long do you figure this is all going to take? I mean, after those cows are sent into the tunnels how long before we know if it's successful?"

"It's a little past eight now," McNeal said, looking at his watch. "Good or bad, we should know by three o'-clock this afternoon." He took a long swallow of coffee and picked up another doughnut. "The way it was explained to me, this stuff attacks and kills the spiders within a matter of hours."

"And if this virus doesn't work?"

McNeal gave his a sour look, then went over to where he saw Dr. Benjamin standing off by himself. "Everything will be okay, doctor," he said as reassuringly as he could. "The men have been briefed, everything's ready to go. . . ." He couldn't help noting Benjamin's wornout look, his red, tearing eyes. "You're obviously a pretty sick man, doctor. Why even consider going in there yourself?"

"It's just something I feel I want to do." He looked at McNeal seriously. "I don't think anybody would understand better than you my feeling of responsibility for everything that's happened. You expressed the same feelings not so long ago yourself."

"I was wrong," McNeal said quickly. "None of us was responsible, none of us could possibly have suspected at the time what it all meant—"

"If I had done more at the beginning, not been so damn smug—"

"But that's what I'm trying to say. You couldn't have done any more. . . . I brought you some spiders to look at, and based on your knowledge and experience, second to none, you *saw* spiders. You had no reason at the time, none at all, to even imagine that they were what they were."

"But at least I want to do everything *now* that I can to help put an end to this . . . this year-long nightmare—"

"I know you do, doctor, and I respect you for it, but I'm afraid it's been taken out of your hands."

"I suppose you're right, lieutenant." His voice was filled with defeat. "Well, if you'll excuse me, I'd like to be alone for a while, try to pull things together. . . ." He walked away in the direction of the medical van.

Professor Meyers came up to McNeal just then. "There's been a change of plans, lieutenant. The cattle will now be divided into only three groups, so we'll only need three or four men to herd each group as far as possible into the tunnels. The rest of the men you've

234

gotten would only get in the way. So please pick three of your best men and have them report back to me."

"Yes, *sir,*" McNeal said, pleased that he wouldn't have to subject more than a few men to the danger—

Professor Winkler came rushing up. "Meyers! The vial of the virus culture—it's gone . . . we can't find it anywhere. . . ." The two professors rushed off together.

McNeal located the volunteers standing near one of the supply trucks, talking, joking nervously among themselves. "Afraid I have some bad news, for most of you," he said straight-faced. "Head man over there says they're only going to need three of you." He studied the group. "Never mind volunteering. . . . Matheson, Duffy, O'Conner, come with me to Professor Meyers." He turned back to the group, all exchanging relieved looks. "I know the rest of you are disappointed, but I'm sure you'll get over it . . . and by the way, thank you."

He walked the three men over to the medical van, where Meyers briefed them. "Our original plan was to drive the cattle into the tunnel system only two or three per tunnel, spreading them throughout the drainage system and thereby giving the virus a wider dispersal radius. When we thought more about it, we decided this would be both unnecessary and time-consuming. As soon as the spider mass attacks and feeds on the cattle, the virus will spread extremely fast by itself among them." He pointed to Matheson. "The herd will be divided into three groups. You'll drive the first group into the tunnel system, entering at that opening over there." He indicated the opening across from where they were standing. "As soon as he's successful, you"—pointing to O'Conner—"will drive the second group in—and you"—indicating Duffy—"the third."

The cattle were divided into groups of sixteen each, then carefully herded up the shallow embankment and

235

into the entrance to the tunnels. There, two of the groups were allowed to mill around by the entrance while Matheson got ready to start the first group on their journey deep into the tunnel. . . .

DR. BENJAMIN stood for a moment, debating whether or not to tell Christine what he was about to do. He found the question rhetorical; he knew he could never convince her it was the thing to do, and if anything did happen to him, well . . . he believed she would understand. And, as he hoped, if he came out of it okay, he'd have saved her needless upset and misery. . . .

MCNEAL STRUGGLED up the embankment, catching up with the police officer before he disappeared into the tunnel. Looking directly into his eyes, McNeal could easily see the fear and uncertainty the man felt, the nervousness and tension evident on his face. "Matheson," he said, "I'm going to give you a direct order. I expect it to be carried out."

"Yes, sir."

"You drive these damn cows as far into the tunnel as you can. But the first instant you see or hear anything, *anything* at all—you turn your ass around and get the hell out of there fast as you can. You clear on that?"

"Yes, sir. All clear." Matheson allowed himself a grin.

"Matheson, I want to be able to shake your hand an hour from now and congratulate you on a helluva job. I don't enjoy presenting any Medal of Valor to a dead hero's widow." He held out his hand. "Good luck."

McNeal then moved very carefully down the embankment, meeting Dr. Benjamin struggling up toward him.

"I just wanted to wish that officer luck," Benjamin explained in answer to McNeal's quizzical look. What's the officer's name?"

"Matheson," McNeal said, nodding his approval, then continued down the embankment and joined Bryson and the others waiting beside the medical van. . . .

MATHESON HAD not taken more than a dozen steps into the tunnel when he heard his name being called. He turned to see Dr. Benjamin struggling up to meet him.

"There's been another change of plan," Dr. Benjamin said, breathing hard because of the congestion in his chest. "It's been decided that the first herd should be driven by someone with expertise in—well, I'm not going into the reasons. The point is, you've been relieved of this duty, I will drive the cattle into the tunnel—"

"But I just talked to the lieutenant, he didn't say anything about a change of plan, matter of fact—"

"The lieutenant is not in charge here—I am. Now, if I may have that cattle prod, I will get on with it."

"Well, the lieutenant seems to be coming back up here, so if you don't mind, sir, I'd rather get the order from him."

Benjamin glanced over his shoulder and saw McNeal puffing up the embankment toward them. "That will not be necessary," he snapped, snatching the prod from the officer's hand and whipping it across the rump of the trailing cow, causing the entire herd to begin moving forward. In less than a minute Dr. Benjamin and the herd of cows were completely out of sight in the darkness of the tunnel. . . .

"What happened?" McNeal asked, already knowing the answer. He had suddenly suspected Dr. Benjamin's intentions for coming up there, which was the reason he'd come back.

"The professor said there was a change in plan—"

"All right, never mind. I can guess the rest," McNeal

237

said. "Don't worry about it."

"Lieutenant, do . . . do you want me to go in after him?" Matheson asked.

"No. The hell with him. He made his own choice—let him either live or die with it."

The order was given for the other groups of cattle to be moved into the tunnels. McNeal cautioned the other two officers in the same way he had Matheson, ordering them to do nothing foolish and to get out as fast as possible.

DR. BENJAMIN, trying to catch his breath, leaned against the concrete wall. The exertion of beating and prodding the cattle to keep them moving at a fast pace through the tunnel, along with his already weakened condition from the pneumonia, was really wearing on him. He'd felt weak and sick even before he had begun, but now his limbs felt as though they were made of lead, and his already inflamed chest felt painfully raw from the labored breathing.

He rubbed his hand across his tearing eyes, took a deep breath, which ended in a fit of hacking coughs. After another moment he cleared his throat of phlegm and wiped his eyes again. He knew his strength was depleted, that his only chance was to keep moving; if he stopped again, he knew he would collapse.

The cattle were milling around in confusion a few yards down the tunnel. He pushed himself away from the wall, struggled to catch up with them. He whacked the leather prod down across the rump of the trailing cow. The animal let out a bellow of pain and terror, then trotted forward, bumping into the cattle ahead of her and starting them all moving down the tunnel again.

He was sure he had already traveled over a quarter of a mile, but there was no way to be certain. The scraping,

238

clawing sounds he had heard as a mere whisper at the beginning of his journey was now an almost deafening confusion of noises echoing through the tunnel ahead of him. He knew he was getting close.

The cattle were becoming increasingly skittish the farther they traveled into the tunnel, and it had gotten to the point where he had to beat them constantly with the prod just to keep them moving. Even then, their pace had considerably slowed.

As he came to an intersection in the tunnels, he stopped to listen. A loud echoing clatter came to him from the direction of both side tunnels but he still could see nothing. He prodded the cattle forward again.

After traveling another fifty yards, he finally saw them, moving quickly toward him like a moving black flood in the tunnel ahead of him. He gave the cows in front of him two more vicious whacks on their rears, then began backing up slowly.

The cattle took a few more unwilling steps forward, then froze in panic. Within seconds, the spider mass had reached them and had swept over them. The unfortunate animals stood frozen in terror.

Dr. Benjamin continued backing slowly up the tunnel as he watched the cattle, watched them as, one by one, their bodies stiffened and they fell over onto their sides, their legs kicking and jerking spastically in death. After that, he could no longer see them as the rushing mass of spiders completely covered them and continued moving up the tunnel toward him.

He turned and began running up the tunnel in the direction he had come from. Suddenly, his escape route was cut off as a flood of spiders came pouring in from the two intersecting tunnels in front of him.

He dug quickly into his right-hand coat pocket and pulled out the vial of virus culture he had taken from the medical van. He threw the vial as hard as he could against the concrete floor in front of him, smashing it, then backed away from the spreading stain it produced. He continued backing up along the wall as the spiders converged on him from both directions.

His hand touched, then closed on, something along the wall, something cold and hard—the metal ladder leading up to the manhole above him. He pulled himself up as the closest spiders clawed at his shoes. He climbed the ladder slowly, not only because of his near-exhausted condition but also because each time he had to use his left hand to pull himself up the stitches on his wrist tore painfully. Fortunately the ladder was mounted on brackets at least a foot from the wall, so that the spiders that followed him up the wall could not quite reach him, though they clawed frantically at him, missing his fingers by a fraction of an inch as he clutched the rungs.

When he reached the top of the ladder he put his back against the steel manhole cover and pushed. It barely moved. Blood now flowed from the torn stitches on his wrist, causing his hand to slip on the smooth metal rung and creating a frenzy of activity below him as it dripped onto the tunnel floor.

Squaring himself as best he could on the topmost rungs of the ladder, he pushed with everything he could muster from his arms and legs, grunting under the strain. The steel cover raised slowly, then slid off his back into the street above him. He scrambled up the ladder and out through the open manhole, quickly pushing the heavy cover back into position over the hole. As it clanged down into position, he noted with satisfaction, it had also severed legs and squashed bodies.

Well, he'd gotten out alive. . . . As he lay in the deserted street, exhausted beyond belief, he said a silent thank you to whatever Supreme Being there might be, then concentrated on controlling his labored breathing and getting back what little strength he had left.

How long he actually lay there he wasn't sure, but after a while he slowly got to his feet and began walking. A boulevard sign told him he was on Colorado Boulevard. He knew if he followed it north he would eventually reach the police cordon at the riverbed. Tying the bandage on his reinjured wrist, he trudged down Colorado Boulevard—back to the living . . . to Christine.

MCNEAL LOOKED at his watch. "It's three-thirty. How much longer we gonna have to sit around? If I drink one more cup of this coffee I'm gonna float away."

"We'll give it another half hour just to be sure," Professor Meyers said. He turned to Professor Winkler. "That would give the virus over six hours to be fully effective. You agree, Henry?"

Winkler shrugged. "If the virus hasn't been effective already, another half hour won't make much difference, will it?"

McNeal noted Dr. Selby sitting by herself a short distance away, got up and stretched, looked at his watch again. Barely five minutes had passed. He took another doughnut out of the carton, his seventh, and began munching it as he started over to her.

He could easily see the worry and tension etched on her face. "Dr. Benjamin's a pretty tough guy, I'm sure he'll be okay. . . ." The look she gave him quickly made clear he'd said the wrong, clumsy thing. "I'm sorry, didn't mean—"

"I know what you meant, lieutenant, and thank you . . . it's just that—"

She was interrupted as a police car, siren blaring, came speeding down the access road across the dry riverbed, to a screeching halt near one of the ambulances. Both officers jumped out quickly.

Christine Selby, sensing what it was all about, got to her feet and rushed over to the ambulance, where the paramedics were just carrying Harold Benjamin from the back seat of the police car and laying him on a stretcher. She went to him, kneeled beside him while the paramedics opened the back door of the ambulance.

He opened his eyes, actually managed a weak smile.

"Harold, you're arm's covered with blood, are you all right?"

He tried to speak but ended up by only nodding that he was.

She turned to the officer who had driven the police car. "Where did you . . . ?"

"He came staggering down the street," the officer said with a shrug. "Told us to drive him here . . . said he had to let someone know he was okay. I'd guess you're the someone."

As the paramedics loaded Harold into the back of the ambulance Christine got in too. Kneeling beside him, she took hold of his hand. "Someone knows you're okay, darling," she whispered.

The ambulance took off, heading for the hospital.

MCNEAL GLANCED at his watch again. Time was dragging. Benjamin was safe, and that was a relief. But there was more at stake here than the life of Dr. Benjamin. . . .

"Impatient, lieutenant?" Meyers asked, climbing out of the medical van and standing beside him.

"You might say, professor. We've been here going on six hours, making a lot of small talk, and yes, I guess I am a little anxious to get on with . . . whatever comes next. By the way, professor, what does come next?"

"We make sure that all the spiders have been eliminated."

"Make sure? How the hell can you make sure they're all dead?"

"By going in there and seeing for ourselves." Meyers pointed to the tunnel entrance. "Coming, lieutenant?"

Go back in there again just to look? Are you nuts? McNeal thought of saying, then thought better of it. "Yeah, that's something I'd kind of like to see for myself." He turned to Bryson. "How about you, Frank? Want to live dangerously?"

"Hell, no . . . but hell, yes," he said, not cracking a smile.

They borrowed a vehicle similar to the one McNeal and Bryson had used the other time they'd gone into the tunnels. This one, of course, had no protective skirt around it, and no tool rack. Instead, it had four bucket seats, which were where they sat, Professors Meyers and Winkler in front, McNeal and Bryson in back.

They went a short distance down the dry riverbed before going up the shallow embankment and into the entrance to the tunnels. As they entered the mouth of the tunnel, McNeal couldn't help feeling a sense of apprehension about going back in, and completely unprotected.

"The tunnels back where we were are blocked with the carcasses of the dead cattle. We would never be able to maneuver the vehicle around them," Meyers said as they started moving into the tunnel. "We'll enter the system through here, then double back to the left."

"If," McNeal said, "we find all the spiders dead in a particular section of the tunnels, do you figure that means they're dead throughout the whole system?"

Meyers thought for a moment. "Yes . . . I'd think so.

I can't imagine how it could be otherwise—"

"What if," McNeal asked, shuddering inwardly at the thought, "we haven't waited long enough for the virus to be fully effective?"

"In that case, lieutenant, none of us will ever get out of these tunnels alive."

As they slowly moved deeper into the tunnel, the usual dank, musty smell of the drainage system was replaced by another odor. It was indefinable at first, sort of a thick, sweet odor that clung to the nostrils. The deeper they went, the stronger, the more nauseating the odor became.

All talk—small and otherwise—had stopped. The four men sat in tense silence, eyes fixed on the sweep of the headlights in front of the vehicle, waiting to catch the first signs of movement. The tunnel was silent as a tomb, the only sounds to be heard the faint whir of the electric motor that powered the vehicle, and the squeal of the extra-wide tires against the concrete floor.

Professor Meyers suddenly released the steering stick, and the vehicle came to an immediate stop. In front of them, just out of the reach of the headlights, a huge, black mass covered the floor of the tunnel.

They sat for a long, chilling minute, watching, listening. No movement could be seen, no sound heard. The tunnel was dead silent, except for the sound of their own heavy breathing.

Meyers looked at the others; they all nodded affirmatively. He pushed the steering stick forward and they began moving slowly ahead again.

It was an endless mass of bodies—bodies lying crumpled and curled on top of other bodies—stretched as far as they could see in the headlight beams in front of them. Millions upon millions of them, covering the floor of the tunnel, or still clinging, in death, to the walls and ceiling.

244

So many their number was beyond comprehension—and this was only one of the tunnels.

"Jesus," was all McNeal could say as he stared in disbelief at the seemingly endless mass of death around him.

As the oversized tires of the vehicle began rolling over the carpet of dead bodies, squashing them, the sickeningly sweet odor became unbearable, and they covered their mouths and noses with handkerchiefs.

The slight vibration from the vehicle rolling through the tunnel caused spiders clinging to the walls and ceiling to drop off. One large spider released its death-grip on the ceiling and dropped into McNeal's lap, scaring the hell out of him.

It took them almost forty-five minutes before they reached the end of the blanket of spider bodies. Finally, they were rolling through deserted tunnel again. Meyers turned left at the next tunnel intersection they came to, traveled in that direction for another hour before turning left again and starting back.

As they made their last turn in the vacant tunnel, a black shape darted through the beam of the headlights, followed quickly by another. The vehicle stopped.

"Did . . . did you see . . . ?" Meyers asked hesitantly.

"You're damn right we saw," McNeal said. "What the hell was it?"

They sat silently and waited . . . for exactly what, they weren't sure. Shortly, another dark shape darted through the headlights and scurried along the wall and out of sight in the darkness.

"Rats!" McNeal said. "Rats are coming in here from other parts of the tunnel system. . . ." He pointed a flashlight down the tunnel in the direction they'd just come from, and the beam picked up tiny pinpoints of light along the walls. Little eyes reflecting the light. They breathed in relief.

245

"Professor, are you satisfied now that we've killed all the spiders?" McNeal asked.

"Satisfied."

"Then I suggest we get the hell out of here. This place gives me, to say the least, the creeps."

They started moving, heading back through the blanket of dead spiders, the way they had come.

"It'll be a real pleasure to go back to work on ordinary minor stuff like murder, rape and kidnapping," McNeal said. "Who knows, I might even face going back on my diet again."

"You won't be doing much of anything for about the next week," Professor Winkler said. "You're both going to be very sick with an acute bronchial congestion . . . that's the way the virus you've both been exposed to will affect you."

"When the hell did we come in contact with the virus?" McNeal asked.

"You're breathing it right now, lieutenant," Winkler said. "But it won't be so bad. You'll stay in bed, drink plenty of fruit juices, take the antibiotic tablets I'm going to give you, and get plenty of sleep. What's so bad about that? A good rest."

"Yeah, not too bad," McNeal conceded.

"Professor Meyers and myself will probably be working with the health department for about the next month, helping to inoculate the city against the virus. That I'm not looking forward to."

They left the mass of dead spiders behind them and drove into the empty tunnel again. Ahead was the entrance to the tunnel system they'd entered by. Beyond that, the bright sunlight.

A LARGE, black rat scurried along the wall in the dark tunnel. It paused for a brief moment and sniffed the air.

It smelled food, and very close. It began scurrying along the wall again.

There was a blur of movement across the floor of the tunnel, and the rat was seized in the grip of strong, sharp claws. It struggled and twisted, but the claws held it tight. Sharp, powerful fangs pierced the back of the rat's neck. It continued to struggle, but more feebly now. Finally, it stopped struggling. Its body stiffened, and it lay still.

The spider held her grip on the rat until she was sure it would struggle no more. She released her death-grip, then began dragging the rat along the wall toward her nest.

She was different from the other spiders, the ones that had died. Her body metabolism and blood chemistry were different from the others', more advanced. She was unique: the virus that had attacked and destroyed all of the others did not affect her.

She had a great deal of difficulty with the rat. Her fat, round body was heavy with eggs, which made her clumsy and her victim cumbersome. Nevertheless, she managed to reach the large crevass in the concrete wall that was her nest and, though with difficulty, managed to pull the rat's body through the vertical opening into the small, jagged cave beyond. Working within the cramped space, she maneuvered the rat's large body into a belly-up position near the rear of the cave.

She would lay her eggs now; the rat's body would provide food for her young.